MW01286635

Tyler and the Twelve Traditions

Other books by Edward Bear

The Dark Night of Recovery

The Seven Deadly Needs

The Seven Deadly Fears

Edward and Tyler: Relapse and Recovery

The Cocktail Cart

www.edwardbear.net

Tyler and the Twelve Traditions:

The Legacy, the Lore, the Wisdom

Edward Bear

White River Press
Amherst, Massachusetts

Tyler and the Twelve Traditions: The Legacy, the Lore, the Wisdom

First published 2004 by M&J Publishing, Denver, Colorado

White River Press edition published October 2010

ISBN: 978-1-935052-30-2

Original book cover design by Sarah Edgell sarah@edgellwork.com

White River Press
P.O. Box 3561
Amherst, Massachusetts 01004
www.whiteriverpress.com

Acknowledgements:
For permission to use the following selections, grateful thanks are extended:
Anonymous. *Twelve Steps and Twelve Traditions*, New York: Alcoholics
Anonymous World Services, Inc. 1952.
Anonymous. *Alcoholics Anonymous*. New York: Alcoholics Anonymous World
Services, Inc. 1955.
Philip Novak. *The World's Wisdom*. New York: Harper Collins.

Author's note: This is a work of fiction. Any resemblance to persons living or
dead, events or locales is entirely coincidental.

Library of Congress Cataloging-in-Publication Data

Bear, Edward, 1933-2006.
Tyler and the twelve traditions : the legacy, the lore, the wisdom / by Edward
Bear.—White River Press ed.
    p. cm.
Originally published: Denver, CO : M&J Pub., c2004.
ISBN 978-1-935052-30-2 (pbk.)
1. Alcoholics Anonymous—Fiction. 2. Twelve-step programs—Fiction.
3. Imaginary conversations. I. Title.
PS3569.L267T95 2010
813'.54—dc22
                                    2010006157

To:

Jo, keeper of the flame.

The children, Tommy, Tree, Cat, Monica, Laura and Steve.

All those who struggle with addictions.

A life spent making mistakes is not only more honorable but more useful than a life spent doing nothing.

George Bernard Shaw

I have never understood why it should be considered derogatory to the Creator to suppose that He has a sense of humor.

William Inge

The Great Spirit is everywhere; he hears whatever is in our minds and hearts, and it is not necessary to speak to Him in a loud voice.

Black Elk

To attain knowledge, add something every day.
To attain wisdom, remove something every day.

The Tao Te Ching

For it is in giving that we receive.
It is in pardoning that we are pardoned.

St. Francis of Assisi

You are a stiff-necked people, uncircumcised in heart and ears…

Saint Stephen, rebuking the Sanhedrin

The highest truth cannot be put into words. Therefore the greatest teacher has nothing to say. He simply gives himself in service and never worries.

The Tao Te Ching

THE TWELVE TRADITIONS OF ALCOHOLICS ANONYMOUS

TRADITION ONE Our common welfare should come first; personal recovery depends upon A.A. unity.

TRADITION TWO For our group purpose there is but one ultimate authority—a loving God as He may express Himself in our group conscience. Our leaders are but trusted servants; they do not govern.

TRADITION THREE The only requirement for A.A. membership is a desire to stop drinking.

TRADITION FOUR Each group should be autonomous except in matters affecting other groups or A.A. as a whole.

TRADITION FIVE Each group has but one primary purpose—to carry its message to the alcoholic who still suffers.

TRADITION SIX An A.A. group ought never endorse, finance, or lend the A.A. name to any related facility or outside enterprise, lest problems of money, property, and prestige divert us from our primary purpose.

TRADITION SEVEN Every A.A. group ought to be fully self-supporting, declining outside contributions.

TRADITION EIGHT Alcoholics Anonymous should remain forever nonprofessional, but our service centers may employ special workers.

TRADITION NINE A.A., as such, ought never be organized; but we may create service boards or committees directly responsible to those they serve.

TRADITION TEN Alcoholics Anonymous has no opinion on outside issues; hence the A.A. name ought never be drawn into public controversy.

TRADITION ELEVEN Our public relations policy is based on attraction rather than promotion; we need always maintain personal anonymity at the level of press, radio, and films.

TRADITION TWELVE Anonymity is the spiritual foundation of all our traditions, ever reminding us to place principles before personalities.

PROLOGUE

The fault, dear Brutus, is not in our stars, but in ourselves...

William Shakespeare

Here I am almost eleven years in recovery, about to marry my One True Love (so it's my fifth One True Love—not everyone gets it right the first time), and Tyler finally returns one of my numerous phone calls. The old Magic Man himself. He Lives. Hallelujah. Sober since the time of the dinosaurs. Every time I call I get his stupid answering machine:

Tyler is on an extended leave of absence and will respond to your most interesting and provocative call when he returns.

Leave of absence from what? He's old. He's retired. He's not out chasing women, unless you count Mercedes, the Vampire. (You may remember her as the *curandera* in The Seven Deadly Fears who plays checkers with God. Tyler knows the weirdest people.) He doesn't have an RV to go traipsing around the country living in trailer parks. What could he possibly be doing? Maybe he's developed an addiction to Bingo and he's tapped out on the Rez someplace. What an image—the Maestro slumped over a Bingo card, praying for just one more spot. *Come on, B3...*

1

When he finally did call back, the conversation went something like this (he just launched into it without any preliminary small talk)…

You know, Edward, I've been thinking…(This is nearly always a bad sign)…*We haven't been through the Twelve Steps in a long time have we.* (Understand that this is not really a question.)

Oh, hasn't been all that long. (Already I'm defensive.)

A year or two you think?

…Oh…maybe…

You know what we really ought to do?

No…what? (Sometimes I could just kick myself for falling into the trap.)

We ought to go through the Twelve Traditions.

And Tyler, that strange combination of Mother Teresa and Rasputin, plagued now with an erratic heartbeat, a bad knee and advancing old age, figures we may not have another opportunity. The shady side of seventy is how he refers to his age, as if he can already hear the Coffin Maker pounding nails in the back room.

He has decided that my best chance for long-term recovery is to go through the Traditions. Which nobody does. Absolutely nobody. I don't know one single person who has gone through the Twelve Traditions like going through the Steps. Not one. (Where does he get these ideas?)

You'll need to know these things. The Traditions are very important. They're a gold mine of vital information. We need to talk about Life, too.

What about Life? I wanted to know.

You know—relationships, hope, prayer, despair, sex, the usual mix.

He's already informed me that I'm his replacement, so I'd better get up to speed. What with Time getting short and so forth. As a matter of fact, several of us are sure that Tyler will never die, that in fact, he's not even human.

…Besides, we need to do another book.

Of course. Another book. Keep him talking long enough and you can eventually get to the Real Reason.

In case you're unfamiliar with the history of these conversations, let me fill you in. It all started about ten years ago with a book called *The Dark Night of Recovery.* I played a lawyer (we decided to call him Lawyer Bob) and Tyler assumed the roll of the All-Wise, All-Knowing Wizard (because he thought it up, he got the juicy part). We met once a week and discussed various things: fears, needs, but mostly the well-known Twelve Steps of the recovery movement. We recorded the conversations, and yours truly, as the aspiring writer, did the grunt work of typing, spell-checking, making sure the files were in the right format and seeing that it got published. In other words, I did all the hard work… and Tyler got far too much credit. My beloved sponsor is not above hogging the limelight from time to time.

Since then, through several more books, I have evolved (maybe morphed) into Edward Bear (which is Winnie-the-Pooh's real name), though Tyler remains the Wizard and I'm still the Straight Man feeding him lines that make him look like a genius (though in all honesty I've been holding my own lately and occasionally getting the best of the exchanges).

And of course he didn't even bother asking why I called, how was my job, my love life, my health, nothing. Just … *Let's get started. You'll need pencils, notebook, tape recorder, the Twelve and Twelve, coffee*…though he informed me that he has to drink decaf now because of his erratic heartbeat. Which tickles me because he used to make fun of people who drank decaf. *Why bother?* is what he said. But I am smart enough not to comment. Hey, I've learned a few things in the last eleven years.

Actually, the reason I called was to check in and see how *he* was. Tyler has a habit of showing up for a few months, then disappearing for months on end. When he's here he goes to meetings, talks to people, he's everywhere. There are Tyler sightings all over town. Then he's gone and nobody sees him. Nobody hears from him. He just disappears. *You seen Tyler? Nope.* And believe me, he's not all that well. So we try to keep track of him. For one thing he still smokes. Thirty-five years in recovery and he puffs his way through at least a pack a day. Maybe more. I call him a spiritual leper, but it doesn't do any good. He tells me he's cutting down. Fat chance. But as bad a time as I give him, I owe him more than I can ever repay.

I do not risk telling him about my One True Love (at least not yet), for fear that he may have something unflattering to say about my choices in life. Especially as they relate to women. Though he is always preaching the doctrine of action, action and more action (*get off the bench and into the game*, he says), he tends to be somewhat critical of my relationship history. *You put names in a hat, and just pick one out to start a relationship with?* Then there's the thing he says about what he considers my unnatural interest in bra sizes, which I won't go into. Not only because it's a little crude, but because it's absolutely false. If you hear it, just remember there's not a shred of truth to it.

Sometimes, after chastising me for some real or imagined transgression, some act he considers a failure to live up to what he calls my considerable potential, he will tell me that he loves me. Then my comeback, my brilliant retaliation which I had been planning since he started talking, my perfectly legitimate defense and counter-attack is of course, shot to hell. What do you say to someone who says, *I love you, Edward. Remember that. It's very important.* What I really think is that it's a deliberate device to keep me off balance, to purposely be disarming so I won't retaliate. Of course he's capable of that. And worse. Don't think Tyler doesn't have a dark side.

So here we go again. I can almost see the Maestro walking through the door, notebook in hand (containing all those quotes he's so fond of), ready to hold court. I'm going to surprise him this year; I have a notebook of my own, in which I too have gathered some pearls of wisdom. He tells me this is to be his Magnum Opus, his most definitive and perhaps final statement. All of which he has said before. We try to make allowances because of his advanced age and fragile ego. But one thing about him—I can always count on him to tell me the truth as he sees it. It might be different from my truth, and I certainly don't always agree, but I listen because more than once it may have saved my life. Don't tell him I said that—he's got enough of an ego problem as it is.

TRADITION ONE

Our common welfare should come first; personal recovery depends upon A.A. unity.

It isn't much fun for One, said Pooh, but Two can stick together.

Winnie-the-Pooh

The meetings took place at my house (yes, I actually have a house now) because Tyler never lets anyone come to his place. We've stopped asking why and now can only speculate, which is probably worse than knowing the real reason. For all we know, he may live in his car.

It took him just one sip of the coffee to generate an opinion. (Tyler's the one who first told me alcoholics and addicts lose everything but their opinions when they finally get into recovery.)

"This is the worst cup of coffee I've ever had," he said.

Which is saying something because anyone who's been in recovery for thirty-five years must have had a lot of bad cups of coffee. I blamed it on the decaf, which I knew would irritate him.

"Decaf, Maestro. What can I say?"

"You actually pay for this stuff?"

I shrugged and repeated the line about decaf. He grumbled a bit, fussed with the notebook he always carries, then looked across the table and smiled.

"So how've you been, Edward?"

6

"Not bad."

"I've missed you."

See? Just when I think I've got him figured out, he surprises me.

"I've missed you, too. Where do you go during your … absences?"

"…What absences?"

"All those times when you don't answer the phone, when nobody sees you."

"Ah, those times…I'm busy doing other things, Edward. Occupied elsewhere, you might say. Shall we get started on our new project?"

"That's it?" I said. "That's the answer? Occupied elsewhere?"

"That's the easy answer. But it's very complicated."

"You out with Mercedes?"

"She joins me from time to time," he said.

"I bet you two make quite a couple."

"We are indeed something to behold."

"She wear her vampire outfit?"

"Only on special occasions."

"Like the midnight horror show?"

"That would be a special occasion."

"She really drink blood?" I said.

"Edward, we've been over this. She's not a vampire. The red tint around her mouth is caused by the V8 juice she drinks in large quantities…Now we ready to start?"

"That all the information I'm going to get?"

"For now," said Tyler. "But it's possible more will be revealed…later."

"Then I'm ready to start."

"Tradition One…"

"Why are we doing the Traditions, Maestro? I mean … nobody does the Traditions."

"That's exactly why we're doing them."

"But there's probably a reason why nobody does them," I said. "Like maybe they're not very important."

"They're principles of group conduct," he said.

"So?"

"What does the First Tradition say?"

"It says..." I had to flip open my notebook and check. "It says...*Our common welfare should come first; personal recovery depends upon A.A. unity.*"

"...Nice notebook."

I couldn't tell whether he really liked it or not.

"Thanks."

"You remember John Donne? The writer?"

"...For whom the bell tolls?"

"Right...It starts out, *No man is an island, entire of itself*...Then later...*Any man's death diminishes me for I am involved in mankind; therefore never send to know for whom the bell tolls. It tolls for thee.*"

"Answer the bell?"

"Close...*If a clod be washed away by the sea, Europe is the less.*"

"Stand together or fall apart?"

"Good," he said. "Now doesn't that seem important? *No man is an island...Any man's death diminishes me...* and... *Personal recovery depends upon A.A. unity...*Maybe without the unity there's no recovery. So recovery's not important?"

"...You think God cares about whether any of us get into recovery?"

"What a question," said Tyler. "You get sober to make God happy?"

"I got sober because my ass was on fire."

"Leave it at that. Personally I don't think it makes much difference how you got here. Or why."

"You think I'm an alcoholic?"

"Doesn't make any difference what I think."

"Maybe I'm not."

"Maybe…But if you're here, perhaps trolling for information, it may mean you have a problem with alcohol."

"But does that mean I'm an alcoholic?"

"You get to decide," he said. "It's a self-diagnosed disease."

"Maybe I'm not an alcoholic and I can go back to drinking. Perhaps even some recreational drug use. Maybe I just had a few bad experiences, a run of bad luck, which coincidentally involved alcohol…and a few other substances." This line of questioning almost always gets him fired up.

"You think that's true?" he said.

I waited a few seconds before I answered.

"…No."

"You've been in recovery now what…twelve years? Eleven?

"Almost eleven."

"And now all of a sudden you're wondering if you're actually an alcoholic? This is a first *Step* issue, not first Tradition."

"Just thinking out loud."

"You trust me?" said Tyler.

"Implicitly. But you may be the only one. I'm not big on trust."

"Good. My opinion, which is worth absolutely nothing in this conversation, is that you're in the right place. People who are not alcoholic don't drink like you did and don't do the things you did. They don't end up at Recovery meetings, and don't spend a lot of time wondering if they're alcoholic. But we can deal with that issue when we get to the Third Tradition. For now, let's deal with the First."

"Okay, Boss."

"Here's the long form of the Tradition…*Each member of Alcoholics Anonymous is but a small part of a great whole. A.A. must continue to live or most of us will surely*

9

die. Hence our common welfare comes first. But individual welfare follows close afterward."

"Circle the wagons?"

"Something like that," said Tyler.

"I'm not much of a joiner."

"Most of us aren't. For all that Life-of-the-Party charade we put on, most of us are not all that socially inclined. So what does, *Our common welfare* mean?"

"It means…our common good, well-being."

"Right," said Tyler. "The commonwealth…a group of people united for some common good or purpose. And what, Edward, would you say the common good is in our case?"

"A no-brainer, Zen Master. And simple…recovery. As it says in the Big Book…*Recovery from a seemingly hopeless state of mind and body.*"

"Precisely. And since at least some alcoholics do come to the conclusion that they can't do it alone, can't get well by themselves, they are literally forced to ask for help. Ask the group, the Community, ask the people who are managing to live clean and sober. They may know something you don't—like how to live a day at a time without drinking. The Community is where you get the Mojo, the Juice.

"If the questions get any harder than this, I'm going to breeze through with flying colors."

"Don't relax quite yet. We need to start slow because…"

"Slow-*ly*, Maestro. Don't forget the adverbs."

"…Thank you, Edward."

"Don't mention it."

"And, in case I forget, remind me that I should never, ever sponsor another writer."

"I'll do that," I said.

"…To continue," said Tyler, shaking his head. "We're starting slow-ly because I don't want to scare you with the tough questions right away. Here's what it says about the First Tradition in the Twelve and Twelve:

*The unity of Alcoholics Anonymous is the most cherished
quality our society has. Our lives, the lives of all to come,
depend squarely upon it."*

"Could be serious business," I said.

"It goes on to say that nobody can be punished *or*
expelled. Plus...nobody can tell you what to do. Imagine.
Everybody is free to think, talk and act as he wishes."

"It actually says that in the Twelve and Twelve?"

"You didn't read it?"

"Was I supposed to?"

"I may have made a really bad assumption. Which was
that if we were going to talk about the First Tradition you'd
at least have read it."

"I probably did," I said. "I just don't remember when."

"But not recently."

"Not...too recently."

"Anyway," said Tyler, "it goes on to say that the alcoholic begins to realize that he is but a small part of a great
whole, and that no personal sacrifice is too great for preser-
vation of the Fellowship. Here's what some poet wrote:

*He findeth not who seeks his own,
The soul is lost that's saved alone.*

"John Greenleaf Whittier," I said. "American Quaker
and poet."

I love that look on his face when I surprise him.

"I'm impressed," he said.

"As well you should be."

"Anyway, the alcoholic learns that the group must
survive or the individual will not."

"No Lone Ranger stuff?" I said.

"No."

"Give me unity or give me death."

"Liberty," he said. "Give me liberty or give me death."

"Isn't that what I said?"

"No...It goes on to say, in one of those *Grapevine* articles that Bill wrote, that an individual with even the slightest interest in sobriety, the most amoral, antisocial, critical alcoholic may gather a few kindred spirits together and announce that a new Alcoholics Anonymous group has been formed. Anti-God, anti-medicine, anti-our recovery program, even anti-each other—these rampant individuals are still an A.A. group if *they say they are*."

"I think I've been to meetings with some of those people."

"And how, you ask, can such a crowd of anarchists function at all?"

"How, I'm asking, can such a crowd of anarchists function at all?"

"I'm glad you asked. The recovery literature tells us that unless we conform to certain spiritual principles, chances are we're *not* going to survive. If we deviate too far, the penalty is swift and sure—we sicken and die."

"A fairly substantial penalty."

"Then we find out that we can't keep it unless we give it away."

"Man...another one of the many paradoxes that are sprinkled throughout the program. Something like *Surrender to win,* or *Give it away in order to keep it.*"

"Indeed. You do Twelve Step work, carry the message, form a group, and make an interesting discovery—most people can't stay clean and sober unless there *is* a group."

"Bummer. That's what I had always hoped to avoid."

"Of course," said Tyler. "That's what most of us hoped. We wanted to be the Lone Stranger riding off into the sunset to wrestle the demons, fight the dragons, and miraculously survive, clean and sober. Orchestra fanfare, please."

"Faster than a speeding bullet, more powerful than a locomotive, able to leap tall buildings in a single bound. It's *Superman!*"

"The Man of Steel; lone survivor from the planet Krypton. And now that the alcoholic has achieved this personal triumph over the demons and the forces of evil, he will graciously tell us how he did it. Trouble is, most loners don't survive to tell about it. Fighting dragons and wrestling with demons can be very tricky."

"I did everything alone," said Edward. "Even sex... Especially sex. I found it a lot safer. Plus, I hardly ever got rejected."

"You have trust issues?" said Tyler.

"No, I don't have trust issues. I just don't trust many people. I have some...problem areas in my life, that's all. I don't think I'd call them issues."

"That's like saying you don't have fear issues—you're just afraid all the time. And notice all the personal pronouns in the First Step and First Tradition. The plural personal pronouns. *We* admitted *we* were powerless over alcohol and *our* lives had become unmanageable. The First Tradition— *Our* common welfare should come first, et cetera."

"It's a we deal?"

"...*Unity is the most cherished quality our society has.*"

"We just covered that," I said.

"I want to be sure you remember it."

"I'll remember."

"It's like the preamble to the Constitution."

"What is?"

"The First Tradition," he said.

"The one that starts out, We the people...?"

"Yeah."

"That's all I remember," I said. "Just, We the people."

"There's more," he said.

"I know that. Jeez, Tyler."

"I'll read it...We, the people, in order to form a more perfect *union*, establish justice, et cetera...provide for the *common* defense and so forth, do ordain and establish this constitution for the United States of America."

"So the Traditions are like the Constitution?"

"They are. Principles of group conduct."

"And you're now going to tell me how they were formed."

"You're a mind reader," said Tyler.

"Only simple, easy-to-read minds." But I smiled when I said it. And so did he.

"…A few years after the Big Book was published, seven years I think, Bill and the old timers decided that, since they were no longer held in bondage to alcohol, their most challenging concern was the future of Alcoholics Anonymous. Hence, *on the anvils of personal experience*, as they said, the Traditions were formed to insure the future of the Community. The glue, as it were, that holds the whole thing together."

"Those guys were pretty smart."

"True. One of their great discoveries was that unless the community survived, most alcoholics would not. The Community, as formed and held together by the Traditions, is the Vehicle that carries us along. Without it, we're stuck by the side of the road hitchhiking and maybe getting a ride from time to time."

"So we need them both," I said. "The Steps *and* the Traditions. One addresses individual conduct, the other group conduct."

"Well said."

"Maybe the Traditions *are* important."

"Who said, *We're going to Never Land, where you'll never have to grow up.*"

"Superman?"

"No," said Tyler, "not Superman."

"I love Superman."

"I know that."

14

"Could be the lady at the Thursday night meeting who's always complaining about how difficult it is for her to set boundaries. On and on. Endlessly. You know, the one who always wears that ratty overcoat...even in the summer. Ninety degrees and she's still got that coat on. I hear one more word about boundaries and I'm going to throw up."

"Ruthie," said Tyler.

"Yeah, that's her. Old Ruthie. Jeez..."

"Personal recovery depends on AA unity."

"I know, but Ruthie...She makes absolutely no sense."

"Not necessary to make sense, Edward. Only necessary to tell your truth, which may or may not make sense to anyone else. The Fellowship decided a long time ago that the only requirement for membership was a desire to stop drinking. Doesn't even say you have to be an alcoholic. Just have a desire to stop drinking."

"But Ruthie..."

"You ever hear her story?"

"...No."

"Ruthie was a street hustler."

"Old Ruthie?"

"You may be surprised to discover, that Ruthie wasn't always old. At one time she was bright and young and very pretty. Turning tricks for booze and drugs. A street whore, if you will. Then there were the mental hospitals and the shock treatments. She hasn't quite retained all her...faculties."

"Man...I didn't know that."

"*Our common welfare*, which includes Ruthie's, *should come first; personal recovery...*"

"*...depends on A.A. unity.*"

"Indeed it does," said Tyler. "Without the Community, all the Ruthies, and there are many of them, all the Ruthies die."

"Less judgment and more compassion?"

"A certain wisdom accompanies the phrase."

"Why do I always seem to be the last to learn?" I said.

"Less judgment and more compassion. For yourself, too."

"I'll keep that in mind."

"For next week," said Tyler, "we'll do the Second Tradition."

*"For our group purpose there is but one ultimate authority—a loving God as He may express Himself in our group conscience. Our leaders are but trusted servants; they do not govern...*Impressed that I knew that?"

"...Stunned," said Tyler.

"And I'm writing stuff in my notebook...For when I take over...I mean after you're...gone."

"I'm not leaving quite yet, Edward. "

"I just want to be prepared."

"A worthy goal...Being prepared. If I'm not mistaken, the Boy Scouts made it their motto."

"I ever tell you I was thrown out of the Boy Scouts?"

"I won't ask why," said Tyler. "I'm guessing that it had something to do with the unauthorized pursuit of Girl Scouts. But don't tell me...So for next week I want you to explore the literature, recovery and otherwise, and come up with examples that best exemplify the Second Tradition."

"Any hints?" I said.

"Read the Tradition in the Twelve and Twelve. Read pages seventy-seven and seventy-eight in *The Language of the Heart*. Then try children's literature, poetry, the Tao, Buddhism, et cetera. Our old friend Rumi may have something of interest to say. Define what *Our group purpose* is... and..."

"Stop already. That's enough...And I need two weeks."

"Granted...But if it takes any longer, I may not be..."

"I know. I know...The shady side of seventy and all that...You should know, Tyler, that there's a large group of people who figure that you may live forever."

"Everybody lives forever," said Tyler.

"…Goodnight, Maestro. By the way, who *did* say, *We're going to Never Land where you'll never have to grow up?*"

"Peter Pan," he said.

"I like it."

"…I figured you would."

"Growing up hasn't turned out to be such a great deal."

"Most of us just get older. A few of the lucky ones grow up."

"You think I just got older?"

"Goodnight," he said. "You might want to try and do something about the coffee."

"…I'll have my people call your people. Maybe we'll do lunch."

"Forget lunch. Work on the Second Tradition."

TRADITION TWO

For our group purpose there is but one ultimate authority—a loving God as He may express Himself in our group conscience. Our leaders are but trusted servants; they do not govern.

Do not seek after truth; merely cease to cherish opinions.

Buddha

"Two weeks is a long time between our meetings," I said. "Let's go back to one week."

"I thought you said you needed an extra week."

"If I had three weeks, I wouldn't get any more done."

"Your wish is granted, Noble Student. Now…What's the Second Tradition all about?"

"I found out what *Our group purpose* is."

"Good start."

"It's Tradition Five…*Each group has but one primary purpose—to carry its message to the alcoholic who still suffers.* A whole tradition about what our group purpose is."

"Truly amazing."

"Amazing that they have a Tradition about it, or amazing that I found it?"

"Both. So what's a group conscience?"

"It's those meetings we have every month. That the groups have. You know—group conscience meetings where they decide things. And why is it I never see you at those meetings?"

"They're... not my deal," he said.

"Meaning?"

"I actually discourage newcomers from going until they've been sober at least a year. You know, all that love and understanding and compassion you hear at meetings begins to vanish when people start talking about making the meeting non-smoking, or deciding if we should start the Saturday meeting at seven instead of seven thirty."

"I even go. Not all the time, but..."

"I know," said Tyler. "And I'm grateful for those who do go. I do my service work in a different arena."

"Institutions?"

"Mostly," said Tyler. "There is a certain nostalgia about going behind the walls and being able to leave when I want to."

"You were locked up for a long time, eh?"

"As I recall it was years. Something like four."

"Did you know that Plastic Man was a reformed criminal?"

"My comic strip hero?" said Tyler.

"He was shot during an attempted robbery at a chemical factory and left to die by his worthless partners. But miraculously, he made his way to a mountain retreat where he got well, and then decided to devote his life to fighting crime. The chemical factory fumes that seeped into his wounds turned him into Plastic Man."

"Talk about a lucky break. What about his sidekick, Woozy Winks?"

"Same deal," I said. "Another reformed criminal who was given exceptional powers because he saved a drowning witch."

"Only in America."

"You never talk about your time in the slammer."

"I know, Edward. Because we're going to write a book about it. You and me. The two of us."

"Really?"

"Really."

"About your prison years? You never told me that."

"I'm telling you now," he said.

"When?"

"All in good time," said Tyler.

"I hope you don't die before we get it finished."

"I'm planning on staying around at least till then."

"You think it'll take a long time?"

"Till I die or till we get the book finished?"

"The book," I said.

"First we have to finish the one we're working on, so we better get..."

"I bet you were like one of the old time gunslingers, Maestro. I can see you as Machine Gun Tyler, the terror of convenience stores and petty cash drawers. The 7-11 Desperado."

"I don't remember that there even *were* 7-11's during my sojourn into the underworld."

"They have banks then?"

"Yes, Edward, they had banks. Banks have been around for a long time."

"Well, no offense intended, but so have you."

"Let's get back to the Tradition," he said. "We can discuss my advanced age some other time."

"Okay." When I sense that I'm pushing him a little too hard, I always try to be agreeable...at least for awhile.

"So we have this one authority," he said, "this Higher Power, this loving Higher Power, who *may*, doesn't say will, who *may* express Himself, or Herself if you're so inclined, in our group conscience."

"This is so one guy can't get on a power trip?"

"We needed some guidelines. As the Recovery Movement grew, we needed some kind of foundation to build on. That's how all the Traditions got started. Let's say somebody wanted to start a meeting in a town that didn't have any meetings. We'll call him Roger."

"You could call him Jesus," I said. "Maybe get more members. Certainly get more readers. There are Christians all over the place."

"That's an outside issue. Check Tradition Ten. So our man Roger gets in touch with hospitals, doctors, policemen, therapists, gets some referrals, and pretty soon he has a meeting that he and a few of his cronies run. Since there are only a few to start with, no need to have elections, so they just appoint the Secretary, Treasurer, and so forth. They decide when and where the meetings take place, what the format is, who makes the coffee, and who chairs the meeting. They didn't have non-smoking meetings in those days so that wasn't a problem. If you were there you were smoking whether you wanted to or not. And they didn't have designer coffee either, regular or useless, although they did have high-energy, red-jelly donuts and other assorted unhealthy snacks."

"You come to the meetings in covered wagons?"

"Cars, Edward. There were cars and banks. We're not talking Stone Age here."

"I can't help myself," I said. "When you start talking about the Old Days, I get a picture of covered wagons and whiskey jugs."

"You remember when Alcoholics Anonymous was founded?"

"I do. June 10th...maybe June 11th, 1935."

"And I was born?"

"Is that a yes/no question or are you looking for an actual date?"

21

"The date. Let me help. It was 1933...And you'll notice that I'm ignoring the sarcasm."

"I'm noticing. And you're also leading by example. I like that. It's not your fault that I have trouble following."

"That's a relief," said Tyler.

"Tell me you're surprised I knew the date A.A. got started."

"I *am* surprised," he said. "Can I safely assume you know about the Washingtonians?"

"Temperance movement in the 1840's. Surely you couldn't have been around when they..."

"No. If you do the math, you'll notice that 1933 comes *after* 1840. I'm just trying to give our readers some historical perspective."

"I get extra credit for knowing about the Washingtonians?"

"No."

"Tyler..."

"Tyler what? You *should* know about the Washingtonians; they're part of your heritage."

"...Did you know that the Dalai Lama was born in 1933?"

"I did know that," he said.

"I wonder if maybe you're the reincarnation of some ancient..."

"To continue...So the new meeting gets started with Roger and his cronies, runs for a year or so until some of the newer members decide they want to have a say in who makes the coffee, who gets the speakers, who decides what time the meetings start. Simple enough, though Roger and his pals don't particularly like the idea of newer people trying to Take Over the meeting, which, they believe, is Just Fine the way it is. So a group conscience meeting is called for the purpose of electing new officers."

"Hurray for the new people. And now this loving God is going to express Himself in our group conscience?"

"*May* express Himself," said Tyler.

"Right. May."

"First of all, it doesn't look good for Roger and his boys. Roger actually tries to load the meeting with friends of his from other meetings, but they're still outnumbered. The New Guys wanted to change lots of things. Roger couldn't figure out what the problem was...*Things been going okay for the last year and a half...Why change...*But the New Guys want a different format, want the meeting times changed for the Saturday *and* the Wednesday night meetings, think Sunday morning ought to be a speaker meeting instead of a step study, and on and on. Roger frankly thinks that besides being a royal pain in the ass, they are also full of shit, and the group conscience meeting was in no way the expression of a Higher Power. Certainly not a loving Higher Power. To him, it's just wrong...*What's the matter with the way it was? Why change anything? It's working just fine.* The entreaty falls on deaf ears."

"The New Guys didn't want to hear it."

"No," said Tyler. "So a vote was held, new officers were installed, meetings times were changed, and Roger and his cronies went down to a crushing defeat."

"Good," I said. "I was for the New Guys anyway."

"Sometimes this precipitates an open revolt with Roger and his boys picking up their marbles, buying a coffee pot and starting another meeting where things will be done the Right Way. Which is, of course, Their Way. Sometimes they take the meeting coffee pot with them, because they-bought it-with-their-own-money, and the New Guys have to get their own."

"Raw deal?"

"Maybe. But that's how A.A. spread in the early days," said Tyler. "Still does A coffee pot and a resentment."

"So how does *A loving God as He may express Himself in our group conscience* fit into this scenario? Surely Roger didn't think that God was expressing Himself in that particular group conscience."

"It may take awhile before Roger gets to that. There is a great story about Bill when he was offered a job at Towns Hospital. Charlie Towns was going to give him an office, pay him a salary, and cut him in on a healthy slice of the profits. He wanted Bill to become a lay therapist, employed by the hospital to bring clients in. *Who better than you*, said Charlie, *the guy who started the whole thing*. Bill thought it was a grand idea, absolutely grand, but when he presented the idea to his home group, they were less than enthusiastic. They saw a dangerous precedent being set—money, property and prestige. The group conscience spoke, and Bill acknowledged their collective wisdom and realized that his plan wasn't the best one."

"You think Roger was considering how wonderful the group conscience was when he was trying to find a church basement or storefront where he could have a couple of meetings a week?"

"Probably not," said Tyler. "But he will eventually acknowledge the wisdom of the move. Maybe he'll realize that another meeting was needed in a different part of town, or he'll end up sponsoring somebody who needed a guy just like Roger. Maybe he ends up meeting the love of his life, getting married and living happily ever after."

"This is the Recovery Movement, Maestro, not the Cinderella story."

"It happens," he said.

"But here's the big question, O Fearless One. How do you know it's God's will that's being expressed in the group conscience?"

"You think we should get the instructions on stone tablets to verify the source?"

"That would probably help. But, barring that, shouldn't there be some way to determine whether it's this Higher

Power speaking through the group, or maybe just Roger's own power-driven agenda? Or maybe the New Guys with *their* own selfish agenda."

"It turns out that the wisdom of the group nearly always proves itself a far better guide than an individual member, no matter how good or how wise he or she may be."

"I'd feel more comfortable with the tablets."

"Faith, Edward. Faith. So now we deal with the last part of the Tradition: *Our leaders are but trusted servants; they do not govern.*"

"Nobody told Roger. He thought he was the governor."

"He did indeed. Turned out he wasn't. The group conscience took over, the eternal wisdom of the Great Pumpkin spoke and he was out of office. It has a biblical precedent...*He who exalts himself shall be humbled, and vice versa*. Matthew 23:12."

"The Bible, Maestro?"

"I believe the Book of Matthew is in the Bible."

"But *you* and the Bible? *That* Bible? I can't believe it."

"I may have been hasty some years ago when I discarded the bath water *and* the baby."

"Man...What next?"

"You should stay tuned, Edward, and try not to be as stubborn as I've been about...certain things. Because I didn't like some of it, I discarded all of it. Another symptom of the No-Middle-Ground Approach I've had about far too many things. I'm trying to work on being less extreme."

"This comes as something of a revelation," I said. "Can we attribute this sudden change to the realization that you actually *are* on the shady side of seventy? Perhaps causing you to reevaluate and maybe even change your position on a certain major religious belief system?"

"*All is changing save the law of change.*"

"Heraclitus."

"Very good," said Tyler.

25

"Thank you. Oddly enough, I've been reading Heraclitus lately. I'm going to use it at your funeral…

They told me, Heraclitus, they told me you were dead.
They brought me bitter news to hear and bitter tears
to shed.
I wept as I remembered, how often you and I
Had tired the sun with talking, and sent it down the
sky…

"You've already prepared my funeral oration?"

"Just some of it. It's probably bad luck to get it ready too soon. But how would it look if I was called on to say a few words and I couldn't come up with anything… appropriate to mark the occasion?"

"As my able replacement, it would possibly put you in a rather poor light."

"See?" I said. "So I figured I'd have something ready."

"Let's leave that for a later discussion. For now, you can explain to me what the last part of the Tradition means: *Our leaders are but trusted servants; they do not govern.*"

"I had to go to the dictionary for some definitions."

"Good place to go for definitions."

"First of all, to govern means, among other things—*To exercise authority over…to control and direct.* Now already we have a contradiction. To be a leader means of course to lead, and to be a servant means to basically be a follower … someone who serves."

"Go on."

"So if our leaders are but trusted servants who do not govern, who does?"

"Think about the Tradition."

Slowly the light went on. Sometimes I'm nowhere near as swift as I think I am.

"Of course," I said. "The ultimate authority. A loving God as He may express Himself in our group conscience."

"Bravo," he said. "One of the definitions of a servant is someone who performs duties for an employer."

"Who is, of course, The Great Pumpkin. But this can't mean that the group conscience is infallible."

"No," said Tyler. "For a good example of a group conscience gone somewhat off-kilter, just think of what happened to the Ninth Street meeting."

"Right. First they did away with the donuts. You remember those chocolate-covered donuts?"

"World-class," said Tyler.

"God, they were good. Now they have celery stalks and dip for refreshments. Celery stalks and *dip*, for chrissakes. And of course they only serve decaf coffee."

"And tea. Don't forget the tea. And it's non-smoking now; how can you smoke in the presence of herb tea? Or celery stalks."

"Impossible."

"But understand that not everyone is unhappy with the new Ninth Street meeting. There are those who are delighted with the new arrangements. The health advocates are pleased. They love it. They voted it in. They think the Second Tradition is working just as it's supposed to…As far as they're concerned, a loving God *did* express Himself in their group conscience."

"It was a bad idea."

"Your opinion, Edward. And valued as such. But just because I judge it to be wrong, doesn't mean it's actually wrong. I'm not the final arbiter."

"Who is…Or what is?"

"Meetings that don't do what they're supposed to do, which is carry the message, eventually just die. People stop going and pretty soon the meeting stops being a meeting because nobody goes. Now even those meetings you don't think much of, like the upscale meetings on the other side of town, continue to draw big crowds because…because why, Noble Student?"

"Because they're carrying the message?"

"A-plus," he said. "You see, rich drunks are just like poor drunks. Women drunks are just like men drunks. Notice the common denominator—drunks. Differences in style, money, beliefs, sexual preference don't make any difference …But we'll save the rest for the Third Tradition—*The only requirement for membership is a desire to stop drinking.*"

"Amen…We're meeting in a week?"

"A week it is."

"Can we do the prison novel in between?"

"Patience, my man."

"I'd really like to get started."

"And so we shall," he said. "But not right now. You might want to go home and write a gratitude list, making note of the things you have, rather than the things you don't have."

"I'm grateful we're going to be doing the prison book soon."

"…That's a start, Edward. That's a start."

TRADITION THREE

The only requirement for A.A. membership is a desire to stop drinking.

In order to carry the principle of inclusiveness and tolerance still further, we make no religious requirement of anybody.

Bill W Letter (1940)

"I've decided that this is my favorite Tradition," I said. "Simple and to the point." "It doesn't even say you have to be alcoholic. Or believe in God."

"No," said Tyler. "Just says have a desire to stop drinking. In the Foreword to the first edition of the Big Book, it said *honest* desire, but they soon realized that perhaps that was asking a little too much. People new to recovery, at least most people new to recovery, have only a nodding acquaintance with honesty."

"So I get to be a member if I say I am."

"You do. It's like those Outback Restaurant commercials: no rules. Steps, yes. Rules, no. Except maybe Rule 62."

"Don't take yourself too damn seriously?"

"That's the one...And no matter how sick and twisted you are, we can't deny you entrance into A.A. You see, if there isn't room for everybody, there isn't room for anybody."

"Who said that?"

"I did."

"Man...What an outfit this is."

"Of course it wasn't always that way; originally there were lots of rules."

"Because?" I said.

"Because they were afraid. They were clinging to this fragile ship called Sobriety and they were afraid it was going to sink if they let just anybody on board. What if they let the wrong kind of people in?"

"Who were the wrong kinds of people?"

"I thought you were going to read each Tradition before we talked about it," said Tyler.

"I did, Maestro. I always follow instructions. You know that. I just don't retain a lot of the stuff I read. It goes back to my childhood. I may have been dyslexic. I think my mother said something about that."

"You just make that up?"

"Not too convincing, eh?" I said.

"No."

"…Truth is, I read it but I can't remember what it said."

"What about your new notebook…that's just like mine? Except that it doesn't have any writing in it."

"Not true. It *does* have writing in it. Some writing. I even have some writing about the Traditions…gleaned from other, esoteric sources."

"I'll withhold judgment," he said.

"Isn't the Need to Judge one of the Seven Deadly Needs, Maestro?"

"…That's why I'm withholding it," he said.

He's quick sometimes.

"So who were the wrong kinds of people?"

"Anybody who wasn't a pure alcoholic," said Tyler.

"I remember now. But what was their definition of a pure alcoholic?"

"That's an alcoholic with no other complications in his life. Or her life."

"No such thing?" I ventured.

"That's what they discovered. Alcoholics often come from the worst possible circumstances, with lots of additional baggage. There's a list of people in the Twelve and Twelve that they thought it would be wise to exclude. I've got it right here."

"I knew you would."

"Page 144...Beggars, tramps, asylum inmates, prisoners, queers, plain crackpots and fallen women were definitely out."

"Queers and fallen women? Come on, Maestro."

"Think of the times, Edward. It was the late forties; that was the standard verbal currency. And they worried about what people would say if they admitted those odd ones."

"They just wanted normal, disgusting, smelly, puking, pure alcoholics."

"Sounds almost quaint today, doesn't it? But they readily admit their intolerance and chalk it up to fear which, they believe, is the basis of all intolerance."

"That might be true."

"See, you're learning already. Open your notebook and write it down—*Fear is the basis of all intolerance.* You'll possibly need to share that with somebody someday."

I did as I was told.

"Just imagine," I said, "if we had actually excluded all those people, we could hold the meetings in a phone booth."

"With room to spare. I certainly would have been excluded."

"Me, too."

"And if the Twelve and Twelve had been written a decade earlier," said Tyler, "possibly *all* women would have been excluded. Never mind just fallen women."

"Oh, bad deal. No women."

"You ever wonder what fallen women really means? I mean did they fall off the pedestal we put them on? Or were they fallin' down drunk? Was it a fall from grace? A fall from favor? Here's a pop quiz question, Noble Student. Who was the first woman in A.A. and when did she get sober?"

"Easy, Maestro. Marty Mann, 1939. She wasn't actually the first women; she was just the first woman who stayed sober for any length of time."

"That will be factored into your grade for this session … which, by the way, is not too high at the moment."

"But…"

"There was a time when people didn't believe that women could be drunks."

"Is this a great country or what?" I said. "Little did they know."

"There is the story about the wives of the men in one of the original Cleveland groups barring women who tried to get into meetings. They had a saying…*Under every skirt, there's a slip.*"

"Tough babes. But then, being married to an alcoholic probably generates a certain type of mentality that may be less than generous at times."

"True."

"What about people of color?" I said.

"Same thing. Early on, the recovery movement was, to cast it in the best light, cautious about such things. Bill was roundly criticized for bringing two African Americans to a meeting in New York in 1940. In some areas they were granted special status to attend meetings as visitors or observers."

"Let's hear it for civil rights."

"Slow as they were, they were probably ahead of the rest of the country. But the women had it worse. There was a Grapevine article in 1945 that gives you a clue about how women were perceived in the early days. That's close to a decade after A.A. was started. Among the perceptions:

So many women want to run things. Too many women don't like women. Many women form attachments that are too intense—bordering on the emotional."

"God save us from attachments," I said. "And emotions."

"Women talk too much. A lot of women are attention-demanders. Women's feelings get hurt too often. Few women can think in the abstract."

"Is the ability to think in the abstract a good thing or a bad thing?" I said.

"I don't have any idea," said Tyler. "It seems like such an odd criticism. What difference could it possibly make if women could think in the abstract or not? It would almost seem like an advantage *not* to think in the abstract. God save us from the theoreticians."

"And what difference would it make if they were too intense—bordering on the emotional."

"Here's Dr. Bob upstairs in his house in Akron having people get down on their knees and give their life to God, maybe even Jesus, and some guy is writing that women might be too emotional. Ever have someone ask, *How do you think*, Edward?"

"Not that I recall."

"It's always how do you *feel*. And what's the thing that's the genesis of all forms of spiritual disease, the thing that destroys more alcoholics than anything else?"

"Resentment, of course."

"Bravo. You're up to a C-plus for the session. Resentment is the number one offender. And resentment is a what, Edward?"

"Resentment's a feeling, Maestro. We've been over this issue before. You actually had me write about it."

"I know, but it's worth repeating."

"We don't want to bore our readers," I said. "Our limited fan base may only have so much tolerance for repetition."

"I'm taking that into consideration," said Tyler, "though repetition is one of the ways we learn."

"So here we have a worldwide community with thousands of members that has no membership rules, that allows anybody in who says he's an alcoholic, no matter how screwed up he or she may be. Ex-convicts and policemen, plumbers, lawyers, priests, atheists, anybody. Eventually even women and people of color. And it doesn't cost a thing; there are no dues or fees."

"Crazy, eh?" said Tyler. "I often think of it as something like The Theater of the Absurd. I got sober in L.A. in the late sixties and at some meetings the people looked like they came straight out of a Fellini movie. Central casting maybe. Women with black lipstick and black fingernail polish, ironed white hair, biker guys with long hair and bad attitudes, Viet Nam vets just back from the jungles trying to shake drug and alcohol problems."

"My kind of people," I said.

"We even had a few streakers when that was a fad. The biggest meeting in town was the Sunday night Wilshire/Normandy meeting. Three hundred people maybe. One night three guys streaked the meeting about halfway through the main speaker's talk. Each one had a word written in what looked like lipstick across his backside:

KEEP COMING BACK.

"I would have fit right in."

"You would have, though the Olde Tymers were not pleased with that particular demonstration. Read some of Bill's Grapevine articles from the late forties. He talks about the sick alcoholic being a rebel at heart. A nonconformist. A no-rules guy. They didn't want to put obstacles in his way, make him jump through hoops to get in."

"This really is a free deal."

"You've already paid your dues by the time you get here. They wanted it known that there were no conditions, nothing you had to do, nothing you had to believe. You can get up at the podium every night and say that God sucks and there isn't anything they can do. You might disturb a few people and set some heads to wagging, maybe send some people to other meetings, but nobody is going to infringe on your freedom to say it. Part of the format in a meeting I used to go to was, *If you are offended by explicit language, we urge you to seek milder meetings.*"

"Listener beware?"

"Indeed. In one of his Grapevine articles Bill says, *In Alcoholics Anonymous, there are no musts.*"

"...Now you're really on dangerous ground, Maestro. You're about to become even more controversial than usual. This may put you in the heretic class. There *are* musts in the Big Book. I heard a guy one night say there were sixty-seven *musts* in the first 164 pages. And he knew because he had counted them."

"The Big Book was written when?"

"Published in 1939, probably finished the year before."

"This article in the Grapevine was written in 1948, maybe ten years after the Big Book. Maybe he thought he needed to soften the approach."

"But what does it mean—*there are no musts?*"

"Good question," said Tyler. "Is *must* a command, a request, or just something you ought to do?"

"My guess is that most people think it's a command."

"Maybe...Does it mean that you can do just as you please; that you don't have to read the book, work the steps or do service work if you don't want to? That you don't have to go to meetings if you don't feel like it? That you can continue to act like a total jerk and still refrain from drinking or ingesting those mind-altering drugs you're so fond of?"

"Well...What's the caveat?"

"The caveat, Noble Student, the warning on the label would suggest that although there are no musts, there are

things that you should consider doing if you are at all interested in staying alive and living a life free of alcohol."

"So the consequences of ignoring all the...suggestions?"

"That's the right word—suggestions. Remember...*Our
book is meant to be suggestive only.*"

"And the consequences are...?"

"You slip back into the mire and madness that is
alcoholism."

"What about the people who just stumble in...get sober
and somehow stay sober? I mean no program, no steps, only
an occasional meeting. What about them?"

"Nobody's keeping attendance records," said Tyler,
"though your chances of staying sober increase consider-
ably if you get involved in the Process. But nobody's going
to insist that you go to a certain number of meetings every
week. We're talking about the Third Tradition, *The only
requirement for membership,* et cetera. Meaning that there
are no religious, social, racial, or psychological barriers in
place to keep people from becoming members of Alcoholics
Anonymous. Or Narcotics Anonymous, or Overeaters
Anonymous or any of the other programs that use the Twelve
Step format."

"Those guys in Rational Recovery don't like us."

"...What brought that on?"

"I was reading some of their literature at the Tattered
Cover the other day. They think we're a cult."

"You think they're right?"

"I looked it up in the dictionary and wrote down a couple
of definitions."

"In your notebook...that's just like mine."

"One is, *a system of religious beliefs and rituals...*"

"Which could apply to any spiritual quest," said Tyler.

"Right...Then there's...*a religion regarded as extreme
or unorthodox.*"

"Like the Greek Unorthodox."

"But here's the clincher...*a usually nonscientific method claimed by its founder to have exclusive power to cure a particular disease.* Or in this case found*ers*, since there were two of them."

"That fit?" said Tyler. "...Maybe." "Except that nobody ever said they had exclusive power to do anything. The disclaimer occurs on page 164 of the Big Book. We just talked about it...*Our book is meant to be suggestive only. We realize we know only a little. God will constantly disclose more to you and to us.* And of course later when Bill says, *There are no musts in Alcoholics Anonymous.*"

"What do we think of the people in Rational Recovery?"

"We don't have an opinion about the people in Rational Recovery. We'll get to that in Tradition Ten."

"I have an opinion," I said.

"You're allowed. It's just that A.A. doesn't have an opinion. You're not A.A.—you're just a member. We are simply happy when anybody suffering from alcoholism or any of the other *isms* gets sober, or slim, or solvent, or free from whatever addiction is presently controlling their lives. People get clean and sober in Rational Recovery. People get clean and sober in churches, synagogues, therapists' offices, schoolrooms, and church basements. Many a lapsed Catholic has discovered God in the basement of a Protestant Church."

"That you?" I said.

"It pains me to admit that there may be some truth to it."

"Why would it pain you?"

"I was brought up to believe that the Church of Rome was the one, true, holy, catholic and apostolic church. The only one; the rest were imposters. We had lots of membership rules and...guidelines. We weren't allowed to even read the St. James version of the Bible. That was what the Other Guys read, therefore unacceptable. We had our own special version, the Douay Bible—the right one. What could Protestants possibly know?"

"But they let you join early," I said. "The church did."

"Right. I was about ten days old when I joined, though I'm not sure I understood all the membership rules at the time. First they did the circumcision thing, and then, adding insult to injury, they baptized me."

"Weren't we just talking about resentments?"

"I'm over it," said Tyler. "I mean if you're talking about me and the Catholic Church."

"…You sure?"

"I've done the inventory and made the amends for my part in it."

"Who did you make your amends to?

"The Pope."

"You made your amends to the Pope?"

"Who better? He's the top guy."

"…How?"

"I wrote him a letter and said that I wanted to make amends for bad-mouthing the church all these years. I had actually stopped doing it and if he could think of anything I could do to make it right, I'd gladly entertain any thoughts he had on the matter."

"You wrote that to the Pope?"

"I did," he said.

"How long ago?"

"Oh, must be ten years now."

"Where'd you send it?"

"The Pope, care of the Vatican. I mean how many Popes can there be in the Vatican?"

"You ever hear back?"

"Not yet."

"You think you will?"

"I haven't given up hope," he said. "But let's get back to the Third Tradition."

"And how you found God in the basement of a Protestant church."

"We can leave that part out. You understand the Tradition?"

"I believe so."

"Then we can safely move on to Tradition Four…*Each group should be autonomous except in matters affecting other groups or A.A. as a whole.*"

"I should do some reading," I said.

"You should. I'm expecting more…supportive testimony from other sources."

"I'm just getting warmed up."

"I hope so," said Tyler. "I'd hate to think this was your top speed."

"…Tyler."

TRADITION FOUR

Each group should be autonomous except in matters affecting other groups or A.A. as a whole.

Sobriety had to be its sole objective. In all other respects there was perfect freedom...Every group had the right to be wrong.

Twelve Steps and Twelve Traditions

"I don't get it," I said. "In the First Tradition we say that personal recovery depends on A.A. unity and now we say that each group can do anything it wants."

"*...Except in matters affecting other groups or A.A. as a whole.*"

"That's what I said."

"No contradiction, Star Pupil. You remember the long form of the First Tradition?"

"Vaguely."

"*Each member of Alcoholics Anonymous is but a small part of a great whole. A.A. must continue to live or most of us will surely die. Hence, our common welfare comes first. But individual welfare follows close afterward.*"

"I knew that."

"But you just forgot," said Tyler.

"...Forgot what?"

"Never mind...The long form of the Fourth Tradition suggests that when groups make plans that concern the welfare of other groups, those groups should be consulted.

It's known as the Principle of Consultation, something that few of us are acquainted with."

"Like talking to each other?"

"That's close," he said.

"I've always used the My-Way-Or-The-Highway Principle."

"As have most of us. It goes on to say that no group, individual or entity should ever take any action that would affect A.A. as a whole…On such issues our common welfare comes first."

"I absolutely and totally agree." I do that sometimes just to get a reaction.

"Amazing," said Tyler. "The light goes on. All is not lost. Allah be praised."

"Considering the world situation, Maestro, this is probably not a good time to be praising Allah."

"A rose by any other name, Edward. We could just as easily have said, *The Great Pumpkin be praised*."

"Which probably would have been better."

"Why?"

I should know better than to get him sidetracked on some controversial issue.

"Let's get back to the Tradition."

"You remember my favorite A.A. saying?" he said.

"I do…*God's will for me is trial and error*."

"Well, that's the way all the Traditions were formed—trial and error. And this one's no different."

"Hardly a comforting scenario."

"It's like road testing an experimental car. It breaks down, you fix it. It breaks down again, you fix it again. On and on until you end up with a car that's pretty reliable. Like the Chinese proverb: *You learn to walk by falling down*. All that trial and error business eventually brought us to the place where Bill W believed that an A.A. group could withstand almost anything. You see, Trial and Error in this case is a method of learning guided by a Higher Power, that loving Higher Power we talked about in the Second Tradition."

"Which doesn't mean we don't make mistakes."

"No," said Tyler. "But hopefully we learn from them."

"I always wondered why, if this Power we talk about knew the best course of action in the beginning, why He didn't just let us know early on and save us all the grief of a Trial and Error process."

"You don't want choices?"

"I want the *right* choices."

"How would you know the right choices if you didn't experiment and see which ones might be wrong."

"By the Trial and Error method?" I said.

"Of course. Would you really want to know the right answers? I mean all the time?"

"Maybe not all the time. Just on life-threatening issues."

"Like romance and finance?" said Tyler.

"They could be life-threatening. I've seen that. I have personal experience about things like that. Besides, isn't this Power supposed to know everything? I mean isn't It omniscient, omnipresent...all-everything? The biggest of all Kahunas? It could actually keep us from making serious errors."

"So you don't like free will?" said Tyler.

"Of course I like free will. Who doesn't like free will?"

"Free will means that you have choices, some of which may include miscalculations or errors in judgment. That's how we learn. You could have been born a cow and then you'd never have to worry about making choices. The Cow God would make them for you. Cows give milk; at least milk cows do. They don't have choices. Our Guernsey, who art in Pasture..."

"Tyler..."

"Sometimes, Noble Student, you have to carry things to their illogical extreme before you can get the full flavor of what you're suggesting. *Reductio ad absurdum.*

"There's nothing illogical about wanting this loving, as you suggest, this loving Higher Power to hint at better possible solutions than the ones I've been making. I need help."

"You'd like an email with choices numbered one through five?"

"…That might work. You know I've had this manuscript, this short story that I've been sending around for almost two years. You remember, the one about the midget and the trapeze artist?"

"That the one about sex in high and low places?"

"That's not exactly accurate, Maestro. You make it sound like pornography."

"Sorry."

"Well, I tried The New Yorker, The Atlantic Monthly, Harper's, all the biggies. Now I'm down to small colleges and independent presses that either don't pay anything or give you a free subscription. And believe me, I've asked this loving Higher Power time and time again to let me know the right publisher so I wouldn't have to spend all this money on postage. It would only be a very small favor from a loving Higher Power, but no…."

"How's your morning meditation coming."

He does this stuff all the time: changes the subject and comes up with something different that he wants to talk about. He shifts gears and approaches the issue from an entirely different angle. He thinks it's clever, but I'm on to him. I gave him my best blank stare.

"You remember the morning meditation, don't you?" he said. "Step Eleven: *Sought through prayer and meditation…* You remember that part?"

"I ask about the manuscript. About guidance. That's a prayer. It's called a Prayer of Petition."

"It's also called a Gimme Prayer. Gimme the Right Answer. Similar to the Gimme a Break Prayer which we are nearly all familiar with."

I can only shake my head at such twisted logic.

"Besides," I said, "what does the Eleventh Step have to do with the Fourth Tradition?"

"We're going to detour for a few minutes to examine this issue about choices. Besides, it says somewhere in the literature that the Group, exactly like the individual, must eventually conform to whatever tested principles would guarantee survival. That's Fourth Tradition stuff...Survival, Edward. Choices. That's what we're talking about. Group *and* individual. Traditions *and* Steps. So...Step Eleven?"

"No time. I barely have time to ask about the manuscript."

"What's the first thing you do in the morning?"

"...Pee."

"After that."

"I brush my teeth, have a cup of coffee and read the sports page."

"You see any time in there," said Tyler, "where you could squeeze maybe ten or fifteen minutes for meditation?"

"Not likely. As you know, my new shift at Safeway starts at six in the morning. That's six A.M...probably about the time you and Mercedes are getting home from a Vampire run."

"Notice that I'm not deterred by your clever repartee. I'll repeat the question in case you missed it. Is there any time in your busy morning between peeing, drinking coffee and reading the sports page where you could squeeze in a few minutes of meditation?"

"Due to my new, early-morning responsibilities, I would have to say that chances were not favorable. I have only a few brief moments to ask for guidance regarding my manuscript. But what does the Eleventh Step have to do with choices?"

"Everything," he said. "The Eleventh Step informs us that prayer and meditation are our principle means of conscious contact with God."

"And if we have a conscious contact?"

"One of the Promises from the Big Book is that, *We will intuitively know how to handle situations which used to baffle us.*"

"So this gets back to...what?"

"Choices. Intuition. You'll make better choices."

"If I practice the Eleventh Step."

"Right."

"That really true?"

"Absolutely."

"And if I don't?" I said.

"If you don't you'll probably continue to make all those awful choices you've been making. Like sending the manuscript to The New Yorker."

"What's wrong with sending the manuscript to The New Yorker?"

"Nothing, except that your chances of getting published there are, to put it charitably, very, very small."

"Well, somebody gets published there. Why not me? Besides, all my choices aren't awful. Some maybe. A few."

"Carla?"

"That was a long time ago."

"Last year actually. Last year about this time."

"Was it just last year? Well, Carla was a tragic case of mistaken identity. I mistook her for a person capable of reciprocal love and devotion."

"And...?"

"She was selfish to the core. If I wasn't such a nice guy I'd call her a rotten bitch. All she thought about was herself.

The most self-centered, immature, irresponsible person I've ever known."

"Sounds just like an alcoholic...Don't you think it's strange that you keep getting involved with women who are emotionally unavailable?"

"Oh...I don't know if that's true."

"I do," said Tyler. "You ever wonder why?"

"No. Why would I wonder why?"

"It might prove an interesting pursuit. It might have something to do with patterns of behavior. You keep doing the same thing over and over, expecting different results. Let me give you a hint: It's an inside job."

"...What is?"

"The fact that you frequently get involved with women who are unavailable. What have we been talking about?"

"My choice of women companions. And the Eleventh Step...And the Fourth Tradition. We're all over the map."

"Give it some thought, this thing about your choices of women. Perhaps something to ponder in those predawn hours between the coffee and the sports page when your all-too-brief meditation's not bringing you any real face time with your Higher Power...You know, now that I think about it, I don't recall if you ever made your amends to Carla."

"I distinctly remember that we talked about it. I put her on my amends list."

"Is that the short list, or the long list? And am I to assume that since she's just on-the-list that you haven't actually made your amends?"

"You can assume that, yes. But it's not all on me, Maestro. Just when I got ready to actually make the amends, you disappeared. No messages, no phone calls, no emails. Tyler's just AWOL. Gone for the duration, however long that may be. Much as I hate to admit it, I rely on you for guidance...sometimes. Not often, but sometimes."

"I'm flattered."

"No need to be."

"You should seriously consider doing your amends before you get in any deeper with Sally."

"…Sally?"

"Sally," he said. "The girl you're planning to take hostage."

"Oh…*that* Sally."

How does he find out about these things? My closest friends do not know about Sally. He disappears for nearly four months, during which time I sweep this girl off her feet and propose the ultimate folly of matrimony. She is my One and Only True Love. This time for real. The others, I understand now, were just preliminaries to this—the Main Event. And here comes Tyler ready to douse the scene of premarital bliss with a bucket of cold water.

"You'll have to meet Sally," I said. "She's terrific."

"She's the latest flame that has your wick on fire?"

"She is. But she's different from the others. You'll be surprised."

"Let's hope so…But let me suggest, perhaps just as a starting point, that the reason you end up with women who are emotionally unavailable, is that you may be emotionally unavailable."

"…I'm shocked that you would think that."

"Why?"

"Because I'm very emotionally available. Very. Ask Sally."

"I'd rather ask Carla or Virginia or Emily and whoever the others were."

"I wouldn't call them totally reliable witnesses, Maestro. They were in my life at a time when I may not have been as emotionally available as I am now."

"Possibly," said Tyler "…Did you tell Sally you were afraid of the dark?"

"Why would I tell her I was afraid of the dark? And what does that have to do with being emotionally available?"

"You going to get married in your Superman suit?"

"What's that supposed to mean? By the way, did you know that Superman was brought up in Smallville, Kansas?"

"No," said Tyler.

"And he could fly by the time he was seventeen."

"Couple of drinks, *I* could fly when I was seventeen," he said. "Maybe younger. But to get back to the question. It conveys the concern that you may still think you're bullet-proof, that you think emotional availability is letting her look at your bank account, or telling her what kind of movies you like."

"You're impossible. That's the reason I didn't tell you about her; I was afraid you'd find something wrong with her."

He closed his eyes for a moment; normally not a good sign.

"Let's get back to the Fourth Tradition," he said.

"I agree. We can discuss this later."

"Over a nice cup of decaf."

"When the weather's sunny," I said.

"And perhaps your disposition will match."

(...*Sigh*. See what I have to put up with?)

"So each group," he said, "handles its own affairs unless they affect other groups or A.A. as a whole. You'll notice that all the Traditions are interrelated. This one relates to the Second Tradition and the statement about God being the ultimate authority that guides the group."

"That *may* guide the group."

"Right. That may guide the group."

"So why do some groups fail?"

"Tradition Five: *Each group has but one primary purpose...*"

I filled it in just to let him know I was up to speed.

"*...to carry its message to the alcoholic who still suffers.*"

"Right. And when they stop doing that?"

"Gone?" I said. "No more meeting?"

"That's one of the reasons, the main one, I think, though there are others."

"Like what?"

"Some meetings just don't get off the ground. Bad vibes, bad parking, can't pay the rent, who knows? The point is, there's no need to judge meetings, or criticize them. When they stop helping people recover, for whatever reason, they just get smaller and smaller and finally vanish. It's like the Magna Carta."

"...What is?"

"The Fourth Tradition. The Magna Carta, as I'm sure you'll remember from your English History studies, guaranteed that the King's power would be limited by law. He was forced to recognize that there were certain rights that were not to be infringed."

"Who's the King?"

"Could be anybody," said Tyler.

"I could be the King. I remember a Winnie-the-Pooh poem:

I often wish that I were king,
And then I could do anything."

"You could indeed. Then you could decide how all the meetings would run. You could be sure that none of the meetings would close with the Lord's Prayer since you don't like it, that..."

"You're the one who doesn't like the Lord's Prayer," I said.

"I know, but since you're the King, I'm going to be your advisor."

"Just what I need—you as an advisor."

"You could decide that all the meetings should be participation meetings, or that they all be speaker meetings, or that they all be an hour and a half, or an hour, or that only certain people could talk. You could make sure that Ruthie never rambled on about boundaries. You could outlaw subjects like boundaries, asserting that boundaries didn't really have anything to do with God or whiskey. Just think, you could con*trol* things. *Everything.* You could be the King of A.A."

"Long live the King."

"*Vive le Roi,*" said Tyler.

He has to sneak in a foreign language from time to time to impress people. Personally, I'm not impressed. I think he has a phrase book that he uses.

"But," he continued, "even though the meetings are autonomous, you can't do just anything."

"You can't? I used to go to a meeting where people did the most bizarre things you could imagine. You ever go to the Architects of Adversity meeting?"

"Many years ago."

"You remember the guy who was going through Primal Scream therapy and would just start screaming in the middle of the meeting? He made Ruthie look like Florence Nightingale."

"...Nelson."

"That's him. The funny thing is, nobody ever said anything to him. He'd just scream for maybe ten or fifteen seconds, then quit. We'd all sit around and wait for him to finish, then go on with the meeting like it was perfectly normal to have someone scream like that."

"But he eventually stopped," said Tyler.

"He did."

"I hear he's a circuit speaker now."

"Nelson is?"

"That's what I hear. Maybe that's a training technique for circuit speakers. So, each group is autonomous; they can make up their own rules, and can call themselves an A.A. group as long as they don't have any other affiliation. If the

Architects meeting thought it was okay for Nelson to scream like that, and it didn't affect other groups or A.A. as a whole, then it was okay."

"How about if I start a Drag Queen meeting."

"You could do that."

"Isn't Drag Queen another affiliation?"

"As long as the group has sobriety as its sole objective *and* they don't exclude anybody, it's okay. Go down to Central Office this week and get a copy of the pamphlet— *The A.A. Group.* It's a little like we're saying to the groups— *To thine own self be true*, but use the pamphlet as a guide."

"You know, people thought you had to be a few bricks short of a full load to even go to an Architects meeting."

"But of course you used to go, and I used to go, so what does that say about us?"

"That we're a couple of bricks short of a full load," I said.

"Proving once again," said Tyler, "that we don't get a lot of well people in the rooms. Alcoholics in general are not terribly well-adjusted people anyway. Well-adjusted people don't drink like we did, or do the things that we did. I ever tell you about the time we stole the money out of the Crippled Children's Pond at the Pomona Fair?"

"No. And don't. I'm trying to look up to you as a mentor, as a spiritual guide. I don't want to hear stories like that. I'd rather think of you as a reclusive poet who drank cheap wine in an attic somewhere and wrote bad poetry."

"I wish it had been that simple," he said.

"So do I."

"So next week onward and upward. Tradition Five— *Each group has but one primary purpose—to carry its message to the alcoholic who still suffers.* And do some reading, Edward. References, anecdotes from other sources. I'm beginning to feel like you're not interested."

"I'm interested. But I'm having trouble locating references to the principles we talk about in the Traditions. The Steps were a lot easier."

"Don't give up," he said.

"You kidding? I'm the guy who never gives up."

"Just one of the many things I love about you. Sleep well. Is Sally on the agenda for tonight?"

"Very possibly."

"Then maybe sleep well is not the proper suggestion."

"Goodnight, Maestro. Have a shot of V8 juice for me."

"…I'll try to sneak a drink when Mercedes isn't looking."

TRADITION FIVE

Each group has but one primary purpose—to carry its message to the alcoholic who still suffers.

Let us resist the proud assumption that since God has allowed us to do well in one area we are destined to be a channel of saving grace for everybody.
Alcoholics Anonymous Comes of Age

"How are you and Sally doing?" he said.

"Tradition Five this week?"

"Not so good, eh?"

"What's not so good?"

"You and Sally."

"Oh…We're okay," I said.

"But you'd rather not talk about it."

"True. I'd rather not talk about it."

"You're going to figure it out yourself."

"It's no big thing, Maestro. Just a small disagreement."

"Which you're going to figure out for yourself."

"You just said that."

"I know. That's your cue to either agree or disagree."

"I *am* going to figure it out for myself. There's nothing wrong with that. I'm no dummy, Tyler. I've been down this road before."

"Too often, I'd imagine. And where did your best thinking get you?"

"Oh...Tyler." Sometimes he's just impossible. The only way to get through it is to agree with him. "...Into the swamp with the alligators and finally into recovery. God..."

"Exactly. A good reason to not always trust your thinker, which, for reasons unknown, may not be all that reliable. Various distortions may have crept in when you weren't paying attention, perhaps during your formative years. Always best to discuss ideas and possible solutions before acting. Discuss with other people, not the many voices in your head vying for attention. Safer. Father Tom says that if it's after eleven o'clock at night and you have a really good idea...it's probably not. If nothing else, look in the mirror and say it out loud...*Sally, I think it would be a good idea to move in together before we get married.*"

"How did you know that's what we argued about?"

"Just a lucky guess," said Tyler.

"She's totally unreasonable. She wants to..."

"*Each group has but one primary purpose—to carry its message to the alcoholic who still suffers.*"

"...What gives, Maestro? First you want to talk about it. Then, when I get started, you change the subject."

"Part of my job is to keep you off balance."

"...It is?"

"Yeah. Be sure you don't get too comfortable. You get too comfortable, you get complacent. You don't want that."

"I don't?"

"No," said Tyler. "You want to stay flexible. Alert. You stay alert, some day you'll be able to hear the sound of one hand clapping."

"The Zen Master strikes again, proving beyond a reasonable doubt that long term recovery is not always accompanied by rational thinking. And how did you know that hearing the sound of one hand clapping was one of my boyhood dreams?"

"If you practice the Eleventh Step as suggested, you will one day get a glimpse of a world where two plus two does *not* equal four, where you'll understand that you have to lose your mind to find it, and you will, as it says in the Big Book, *intuitively know how to handle situations which used to baffle you.*"

"Oh boy...another dream come true."

"You remember what Caesar said about Cassius?"

"...Shakespeare?"

"Shakespeare."

"...Something about lean and hungry as I recall."

"*Yon Cassius has a lean and hungry look. He thinks too much; such men are dangerous.*"

"So I think too much?"

"Let me suggest that your thinking, while perhaps not excessive, may be too...inflexible," said Tyler. "Things get too inflexible, too rigid, they break."

"So what happened to Eternal Verities? Truths that never changed."

"*All is changing save the law of change.*"

"God...Confusion reigns."

"Confusion is considered by some to be the beginning of wisdom."

"Not by yours truly."

"The world, Edward, like your recovery, is a work in progress—always changing, always different, always becoming. What was true a hundred years ago may not be true today. Or tomorrow. And, as I'm sure you remember, the Fear of Change is one of the Seven Deadly Fears."

"You know," I said. "I'm not at all sure I'd recognized Truth if it bit me on the ass."

"Seeking is the right action; finding is a bonus. You know—God could and would if *sought*, not found. You run across anybody who has actually found God, you should get away as soon as you can. Your Truth today is that you're an alcoholic with borderline addictions to other substances and behaviors. That's enough Truth for one day."

"You ever think how nice it would be to take a vacation from recovery? Just a weekend. A long weekend. And it wouldn't count as a slip. You wouldn't lose your place in line. Everybody would understand that you just needed a vacation from all that abstinence you'd been practicing."

"You could...indulge yourself," said Tyler.

"And forget about primary purpose for awhile. Relax a little. Let your hair down. You ever think of that?"

"I have thought of that. More than once, as a matter of fact. But then, almost immediately, my mind jumps back to a scene in the felony tank of the Compton City Jail where yours truly is residing due to his inability to play well with others after having a few drinks and a few non-habit-forming pills. Perhaps I ingested an inhaler or two that day. I'd done that before."

"Ugh...You ate inhalers?"

"Not the tastiest of snacks," he conceded, "but it got the job done. The thought process is a little cloudy, but I remember vaguely that, since I was unemployable at the time, it seemed like a perfectly rational decision to relieve someone else of their money. You know, share the wealth."

"Was it after eleven o'clock at night?"

"Actually it wasn't. Might have been better if it had been, perhaps under cover of darkness I would have been less recognizable, but the idea had little merit no matter what time it was."

"You were caught red-handed, as it were."

"And subsequently picked out of a lineup with four others, all under five foot five."

"And at six foot plus you were the obvious choice."

"I was indeed...But, enough of that...If I happened to inquire about your primary purpose today, what would you say?"

"At the moment, it's Sally."

"Honest answer. How about long term, Edward."

"...I'm focusing..."

"The wheels are turning," he said. "I can hear them grinding away."

"Got to be the same as the group—Stay sober and carry the message."

"And the message is?"

"It's possible to live without alcohol or any of its mind-altering companion drugs."

"Wrong," he said.

"...Wrong?"

"Wrong...You remember from your reading I'm sure, the line about, *Shoemaker, stick to thy last.*"

"Followed by...*better to do one thing supremely well than many badly.*" I nailed it again. He never seems to get over being surprised when I do the homework or come up with some killer quote that's right on the money.

"Well done. But we're not carrying the message to drug addicts, or overeaters, or compulsive gamblers. I mean that may happen, but it's not our primary purpose. We're carrying the message to alcoholics who still suffer."

"But it works for those other people."

"It does," said Tyler.

"...So why all the other groups?"

"Because we're carrying the message to the *alcoholic* who still suffers, not the overeater who still suffers, or the drug addict who still suffers, or the gambler...They have their own groups: Gamblers Anonymous, Overeaters Anonymous, Narcotics Anonymous and scores of others."

"Alcohol's a drug."

"True. And many of us had problems with other drugs."

"So?"

"What was the first thing that made you think that Alcoholics Anonymous might work for you?"

"That number I did in elevators was something of a red flag. Bed-wetting certainly got my attention. And the attention of at least one of my ex-wives. Puking on my shoes was another indicator. Blackouts. Waking up in jail. Car wrecks."

"I mean the first thing you heard at a meeting that made you consider the possibility that A.A. might work for you."

"Somebody," I said, "got up and talked about his drinking and it sounded just like mine."

"Identification, right? You recognized a kindred soul."

"I did. A kindred soul who didn't seem all that unhappy about being sober. Which surprised me. I was in jail, I was sober, and I wasn't a bit happy about it."

"What if somebody had gotten up and shared their experience about shooting heroin?"

"I never shot heroin."

"…Or how they couldn't stop eating even though they weighed in at three bills?"

"I'm a shade over two ten. Two twenty tops."

"The point is, you probably wouldn't have identified with the guy who was shooting up, or with someone who was eating a whole apple pie for breakfast."

"Probably not," I said, "though I have had cupcakes for breakfast. A dozen one time—all chocolate. I love chocolate cupcakes. And chocolate donuts. Chocolate anything."

"Hence the need for singleness of purpose. Sober members of the community have this uncanny ability to help other drunks. They don't do as well with gamblers or people with other addictions. No identification. You can't understand why somebody just bet the rent money on some hay burner, and he can't understand why you just don't cut down on your drinking, especially after those two DUI's."

"I had three DUI's."

"I know that," said Tyler. "And did a little time in the County slammer for your transgressions."

"The Honor Farm. I was on the crew that fed the hogs."

"Type casting."

"We used to pick the big slices of baloney and ham out of the slop buckets, wash them off, put them between pieces of bread that we stole from the mess hall and sell them to hungry convicts for fifty cents each."

"Free enterprise," said Tyler. "The American way. A couple more months and you might have been able to retire."

"Well…"

"So, having established that each group has but one primary purpose, the literature goes on to suggest that our ability to carry the message is in no way contingent upon how smart or eloquent we might be."

"That's a relief," I said.

"Seems that the legacies of suffering and of recovery are easily passed on to other alcoholics."

"You know, that's what's so weird."

"What is?"

"I went to my first meeting when I was up on the County Farm. You know, Sheriff Gene's place. And I went because somebody said that if you went and signed the roster sheet, you'd get three days good time off your sentence."

"Did you?"

"I went but didn't get the good time," I said. "Which, of course, really pissed me off."

"I bet. Here you go to all the trouble to go to their lousy meeting and they don't give you the good time. Man…who can you trust?"

"The point is that, even though I didn't get sober for some time after that, I actually believed the guy who spoke that night. I never believed what *any*body said in those days. Especially about drinking. I was stuck in my cocoon of Terminal Uniqueness. But I remember what this guy looked like, even remember his name, and most of his story. He was an ex-convict, old with gray hair. Not unlike you, Maestro."

"Handsome?"

"More beat up looking than handsome."

"Rugged," said Tyler.

"You could say that."

"Could have been me."

"This was twenty years ago, Tyler."

"I was sober twenty years ago."

"I know…but it wasn't you. This guy was old and beat up looking."

"Rugged."

"Beat up and rugged looking twenty years ago. Besides, his name was Marty."

"Probably dead by now," said Tyler.

"Probably."

"But you didn't get sober then."

"No. Had lots of excuses, reasons why I couldn't get sober. Didn't *want* to get sober, though I never actually said that. Too young, too smart, too busy, too…something. There was no way I was going to join this crummy three-drums and-a-whistle spiritual band you guys had going. I figured you guys as strictly lightweight. I was in my twenties, for chrissakes. I had lots to do. Mountains to climb. Worlds to conquer. Intellectual avenues to explore. I was reading Gurdjieff and Ouspensky and trying to get my ouija board to give me some coherent answers."

"And getting a good running start on your illustrious drinking career," he said.

"Yeah…But even though I didn't share a lot of life experiences with this guy who talked, I identified with *how* he drank. Not what he drank or where he drank, but the way he drank. Even then I had that same kind of desperate I've-got-to-have-a-drink mentality."

"Powerless over alcohol," said Tyler. "Life unmanageable. What to do…No way out. What a dilemma. So what happened?"

"I ignored the whole sobriety thing for as long as I could. Went to meetings sporadically. When it suited me."

"And then...?

"You remember a meeting called Joe's Place, in that big church over on Franklin? Franklin and Highland, I think."

"The one they had to close down because the drunks out in the parking lot kept throwing rocks through the stained glass windows...*Take that, God! I'll show You. You and your lousy Recovery meeting.*"

"That's the one," I said. "Well, I happened to drop in one night, filled with my usual quota of angst and despair and... something clicked. For the first time it occurred to me that it might be possible for me to get sober."

"When the pupil is ready, the teacher will be found."

"I thought of that, but..."

"But what?"

"But it didn't make any sense, Maestro. Still doesn't. What was different? I'd been to dozens of meetings. No reason why that particular meeting should be different."

"Why do you always insist on taking a fourth dimensional experience and trying to explain it in three dimensional terms? Of course it didn't make sense. Doesn't make sense. It was crazy wisdom, the wisdom of the spirit. We don't yet have a vocabulary for those kinds of experiences. As more and more people begin to have them, we'll develop one, but for now, you're on your own. You can grunt and smile and those who are familiar with the experience will grunt and smile in return—that way you'll know that they know. From the rest you'll get that thousand-yard stare of total incomprehension."

"It gets more and more mysterious, doesn't it?"

"It does," said Tyler. "But don't get sidetracked by how mysterious it is. As you get deeper into the process, some of your most cherished opinions will be called into question.

You will be forced to discard them and will have no others to take their place."

"That could be called discouraging," I said.

"It could if you didn't have something called a Primary Purpose that keeps you and the group focused on what's important. Understanding will come later. *May* come later."

"We're carrying the message."

"We are."

"I've got some quotes about carrying the message…and being of service. Some are a little far-fetched, but…"

"Just read them, Edward."

"The first one is Albert Schweitzer…*You don't live in a world all your own. Your brothers are here, too.*"

"I assume that includes sisters also," said Tyler.

"Doesn't say, but let's give him the benefit of the doubt. The next one is from somebody I never heard of: Wilfred Grenfell."

"You never heard of him?" said Tyler. "Played for the Red Sox in the early twenties."

"Tyler…Anyway, this is what Wilfred said…*The service we render others is the rent we pay for our room on earth.*"

"I like it," said Tyler.

"This one from Richard Trench…*Ceasing to give, we cease to have; such is the law of love.*"

"Very good, Noble Student. On the order of, *You have to give it away to keep it.* So each group exists to carry the message of recovery…"

"…To those who need it."

"To those who *want* it," said Tyler. "Big difference."

"Amen."

"So for next week we'll discuss the things we *don't* want to get involved in, the things that distract us from our primary purpose. Like money, property and prestige. Tradition Six."

"I'll be ready. By the way, I'm liking this better than I thought I would."

"Was there a little contempt prior to investigation involved?"

"…Maybe."

"Keep moving and watch the scenery change."

"Goodnight, Maestro. Get some sleep. You've been looking awfully tired lately. You even sound tired."

"I'll be answering the bell for the next round anyway. Remember that Somebody is always watching."

"…Who?" I said.

"We're not sure yet."

"Jesus?"

"…Could be. Also could be Buddha. Or Quan Yin. Brahman even."

"Goodnight, Maestro. Try to get some rest."

TRADITION SIX

An A.A. group ought never endorse, finance, or lend the A.A. name to any related facility or outside enterprise, lest problems of money, property, and prestige divert us from our primary purpose.

Great minds have purposes, others have wishes.
Washington Irving

"So what's wrong with money?" I said.

"Who said there was anything wrong with money?"

"That's basically what the Tradition says."

"Careful reading, Star Pupil, will reveal that it simply says the group ought never endorse, finance or lend the A.A. name to anybody, because if they do, problems of money, property and prestige might possibly divert them from their primary purpose. Which is…?"

"You think I forgot already? Like maybe I'm an idiot with no short-term memory."

"You have a nice week?" he said.

"I had a terrible week, but thanks for asking. And I'm not the one with short-term memory loss…You are."

"You're right, I forgot. Which is normal for somebody with short-term memory problems."

"Jesus. Why am I doing this? I feel like a robot that's programmed to answer questions…Primary purpose is to stay sober and help other drunks."

"Commendable. You see, it doesn't say there's anything wrong with money, property or prestige."

"But the original group certainly could have used some money to get started. The way I heard it, nobody had any money in the beginning."

"True," he said. "Bill was an unemployed stockbroker and Dr. Bob, a nearly unemployed proctologist."

"Don't you think it…strange that Dr. Bob was a proctologist. Ironic maybe."

"Somehow, it seems just right. Appropriate may be the word. Anyway, that's probably not the right question to be pursuing at the moment."

"…We're having a terrible time."

"Who is?"

"Me and Sally…We're on the verge of calling the whole thing off."

"We'll talk about it later."

"Later tonight?" I said.

"Later tonight. First, the Tradition."

"Where were we? Oh yeah…money. Don't you think it would have been better, at least in the beginning, if they had some working capital? They could have had a line of soft drinks—A.A. Cola maybe. Or how about Sober Suds, the non-alcoholic beer. Things they could sell so they could get a little seed money to jump-start the process and reach more people."

"They thought exactly the same thing," said Tyler. "They thought that their real problem was that they didn't have enough money. How many of us think the same thing? *If I just had some more dough, I'd be okay.* So they wanted to cash in on A.A.'s marvelous success. The name up in lights:

GET WELL AT THE A.A. HOSPITAL

"And why not public education programs to inform the masses that alcoholism is a disease and that they had the answer, the veritable cure to the problem that had plagued mankind since the beginning of time? Alcoholics wouldn't end up in jail anymore; enlightened judges would send them to A.A. where we'd fix them."

"Big job, fixing drunks."

"Impossible job," he said. "Then, of course, if we could accomplish those worthy goals, why not address other social issues? We could clean up politics, resolve differences between various religions, and straighten out the medical profession."

"Why not an actual political party?" I suggested. "We could have Republicans, Democrats, and us, The Recovery Party. We could solicit campaign contributions. A vote for Recovery is a vote for…what?"

"Ego inflation. A vote for disaster. Might as well call it the Panacea Party. Our campaign slogan could be something like, *We're going to fix Everything, even the things that aren't broken.*"

"You know we could actually do some things to make it a better world."

"We could and we are," said Tyler. "The trouble comes when you incorporate money, property and prestige into the mix. Soon you have drunks running hospitals and schools, dictating public policy. Can you imagine a more frightening nightmare?"

"No."

"Think of Brown Bag Bill running a school. Or maybe worse, a hospital."

"Didn't he do something like that at one time?" I said.

"Hard as it may be to believe, our friend Bill was a corporate guru at one of the big technology companies. Way up on the Food Chain."

"Mister Big."

"Indeed. Before the nosedive into oblivion," said Tyler. "Then he was Mister Little on skid row. Remember his story? Five martini lunches at the SmokeHouse where the martini glasses were as big as Frisbees. That's probably close to a pint of gin. And that was just for lunch."

"The warm-up for the nighttime vigil at the Midnight Mission."

"Greasing the skids, so to speak. But even then the Mission was getting very upscale. They were starting to insist that you had to be sober to get in and get a bed."

"Seems unfair," I offered.

"Absolutely. If I could've gotten sober, I probably could have landed a job and afforded my own hotel room. What happened to the good old days when you could just go in, give them the fifty cents, find a flop and pee in the bed?"

"Like the place, I think it was The Palace Hotel, next to the Rusty Zipper Group where Father Eddy got sober. Finally…"

"Right," said Tyler. "Where the real alcoholics gathered. The Leaky Bladder Boys. You know Eddy runs the diocesan Outreach Program now. Been sober three, maybe four years."

"The Church has an Outreach Program? For priests?"

"They do."

"They've recognized the fact that priests may have drinking problems?"

"Evidently," said Tyler.

"Absolutely amazing. Maybe there is a God."

"Most likely. If I had to wager one way or the other, I'd bet on the yes side. Just in case."

"It may be time for me to go back and embrace Holy Mother Church."

"The Church hasn't progressed that far yet, Edward. You have several ex-wives that may prove to be an impediment."

"Well, maybe someday...Anyway, so Brown Bag lost it all?"

"Then borrowed some more and lost that, too."

"Borrowed more money?"

"Money, credibility, trust," he said. "Whatever he could borrow or leverage, and it all went down the same rat hole. And, although he's now sober, he has managed to retain some of those characteristics that once got him into so much trouble."

"We could maybe call them character defects."

"Possibly...The point being that we probably don't want him running a school or making public policy decisions. Bill loves politics. And being in control. He takes control very seriously. Ever see him at a business meeting or a group conscience meeting?"

"I have."

"He's the first to speak. And often the last. He knows all the procedures, the Rules of Order, everything. He...controls things. And drives people crazy."

"Do I recognize another of the Seven Deadly Needs, Maestro—the Need to Control? Anyway, we'll cross him off the list of hospital administrators."

"So," said Tyler, "they decided that they didn't want A.A. hospitals, or A.A. clubhouses, or A.A. anything. They tried it—didn't work. People got confused. They didn't know if we were in the legal reform business, the medical business, or the political business."

"Yeah," I said, "but it all seems so logical. Why not A.A. hospitals? Who better to carry the message than the members themselves?"

"It does seem logical, doesn't it. And it certainly doesn't stop us from carrying the message. But they discovered, through the usual trial and error method, that they got into trouble when they branched out in other areas. They actually did think about marketing a line of soft drinks, even considered endorsing distilleries that wanted to get in the alcohol education business and use A.A. to legitimize their pitch."

"I can see it now—*A.A. endorses responsible drinking ... of Bud Lite.* Of course we would be handsomely paid for the endorsement...but who would get the money?"

"I would because I thought of it first," said Tyler.

"No, I would because I actually made the pitch on teevee."

"See what I mean? Diversions from our primary purpose."

"Is that what eventually happened to the Washingtonians?"

"It was one of the things. You know at the height of the Washingtonian Movement, in the early 1840's, there were more than 600,000 pledges signed, and thousands of people were marching in temperance parades. They even launched their own newspaper."

"Fast workers. What did the pledges say?"

"Something to the effect that we, the undersigned, pledge ourselves as gentlemen, that we will not drink any liquor, wine or cider."

"No women?"

"No," said Tyler. "It was thought, during those unenlightened days, that women couldn't be alcoholics."

"We've come a long way."

"Equality is just a swallow away."

"I'm glad," I said.

"Glad about what?"

"That we have women alcoholics."

"I bet you are."

69

"And they're coming in younger and younger, before they do all that damage to themselves."

"Why do I suspect your motivation in all this."

"Because you're a grouchy old man who can't stand to see the younger generation having fun."

"Not true. I don't begrudge anyone having fun. What's the one thing the Big Book insists on?"

"Enjoying life," I said.

"I rest my case. But we digress, Noble Student. Let's get back to the Tradition. So they got all these pledges and developed this following in just a few years. Just think—no teevee, no radio, no telephones. Just newspaper and word-of-mouth and they end up with more than a half a million members in just four or five years. It took A.A. that long to get the first one hundred members."

"Yeah, but we're still here almost seventy years later … What kind of a program did they have?"

"Well, they had public confession and public commit-ment. *I did it and I won't do it again*—that sort of thing. They had what we'd call Twelfth Step calls—older members calling on newer members. They often gave newcomers financial assistance, something we seldom do, or do on a very limited basis. Participation in experience-sharing was a part of it, as was working with other drunks and, last but not least, sober entertainment."

"Like dating," I said.

"I don't think that's what they had in mind."

"Dating can be very entertaining."

"Granted," said Tyler. "But I don't think they had dating in mind. This was the early 1840's, Edward."

"So what happened?"

"Five years after the movement started, it was out of gas," said Tyler. "They had no effective way to resolve conflicts as the movement grew. No traditions. No real steps. They discovered that what it takes to sustain sobriety is quite different from what it takes to initiate sobriety. Like, *What happens when the Pink Cloud vanishes?* Steps? What steps? There was no tradition of anonymity, so when one of the better known members fell off the wagon, as happened from time to time, it did substantial damage to their slogan: *A never failing remedy in all stages of the disease.* But for our purposes and the Sixth Tradition, the thing that was most harmful was the fact that they got involved in political controversies. They got distracted. They forgot about the Primary Purpose."

"Stay sober and help other drunks."

"Right. But they had debates about Prohibition, the Wets and the Drys, the moderation guys who were called the Damps, slavery, politics, everything you could think of. Eventually, only a small number of people attracted to the meetings were actually alcoholic. It was said that only ten percent of the 20,000 members of Boston's Washingtonian Society were alcoholics."

"What were the other people doing there? They come for the entertainment?"

"I hadn't thought of that," said Tyler.

"You may be too old to think about entertainment."

"Not true, but that's another issue, Noble Student. Now tell me about the latest problems to hit the Sally and Edward Show."

"Oh…It's the wedding. She wants a Big Wedding. I mean Big. She has hundreds of relatives. Actual blood relatives. Just family, she says, but that's hundreds of people. Should be a limit to how many relatives you're allowed to have."

"You could invite all your ex-wives, maybe even up the count a little bit."

"Very funny."

"And of course you want a little tiny wedding," he said.

"Maybe not so tiny, but reasonable. Dozens, not hundreds."

"She been married before?"

"Once," I said.

"A virtual newcomer to the wedding game. An amateur. Do you have a fallback compromise position?"

"My position is being overrun."

"Time to surrender?"

"...Not yet."

"Tough guys don't give up," said Tyler. "Think Primary Purpose."

"What's that supposed to mean?"

"What's the Primary Purpose of the wedding?"

"To get married, Maestro. What's the Primary Purpose of any wedding? Jeez...What a question."

"Are problems of money, property and prestige diverting you from your Primary Purpose?"

How does he do that? He turns an innocent remark into an attack on my character.

"I have a one-word answer," he continued.

"Which is?"

"Surrender."

"Of course. You think surrender is the answer to everything. Surrender and acceptance, the twin pillars of Recovery."

"We have ceased fighting anything or anyone."

I hate it when he starts quoting the Big Book. It's like Holy Writ to him. That's his final refuge.

"...Okay," I said finally. "I'll...think about it—about surrender. Consider it."

"You've already lost. Might as well be gracious about it."

I grumbled a bit so he'd know I wasn't giving in too easily, but I knew he was right. What're a few hundred people for a wedding, give or take a dozen or two? I wasn't going to win anyway. Primary Purpose indeed.

"Have you managed to recycle some appropriate wisdom from your vast storehouse of spiritual maxims?"

"Hard to find things that apply," I said.

"Try one; we'll make it fit."

"I read one this week that I can't get out of my head. It doesn't have anything to do with the Tradition, but I can't stop thinking about it."

"Let's hear it," said Tyler.

"It's by Elie Wiesel, the Holocaust survivor. You heard of him?"

"Yeah."

"He said, *Don't say anything about God that you're not willing to say while standing over a pit of burning babies.*"

Neither of us spoke for a few moments.

"…You're right," Tyler said finally, "it doesn't fit."

"Don't you find it…odd? Weird maybe."

"The image is so…something. I can't find a word."

Not much shakes him up, but I can tell that this got to him.

"Can you imagine," I said, "standing over a pit of burning babies and saying something about God?"

He just shook his head.

"I heard a story once," he said, "about three rabbis who got together and decided to put God on trial."

"For what?"

"I don't remember. Maybe crimes against humanity. Anyway, it was all very serious. Took two days."

"What was the verdict?"

"Guilty. They decided that God was guilty of whatever they had Him on trial for. But that wasn't the odd part; we could probably put God on trial every day and find Him guilty of something."

"Just to be on the safe side, I don't want to be on the jury."

"The odd part was after they had found Him guilty, the leader of this notable tribunal said, *Now let's go and pray.*"

"…Why?"

"That's the perfect question, isn't it? The answer, I think, is that indifference is the real sin. Love or hate at least acknowledges the existence of the Other. Indifference doesn't."

"I'm sorry I brought it up, Maestro. It's too late to be discussing stuff like this. Anyway, I've got to be going."

"Let me guess—you've got a date with Sally."

"True. I'm going to turn in my sword and surrender."

"You're getting smarter by the minute. Let me leave you with a choice remark by Bill W. In essence, he says, the core of A.A. is one alcoholic talking to another, whether it's on a curbstone, in a home or at a meeting. We don't need a palace or a big clubhouse. It's the message, not the place."

"Amen."

"Go with God."

"Do I have a choice?"

"…No. It just helps to acknowledge it sometimes."

TRADITION SEVEN

*Every A.A. group ought to be fully self-supporting,
declining outside contributions.*

Won't money spoil this thing?

John D. Rockefeller

"Well, did you surrender last week?" said Tyler. "Turn in
your rusty, useless sword to your bride-to-be?"

"I did. Not only that; I turned my entire will and my life
over to her."

"Just the sword probably would have done it."

"I was only following orders."

"Suggestions."

"Right, suggestions."

"I'm not big on orders," he said.

"I know that."

"Feel better?"

"...Relieved." I said.

"That wasn't so hard, was it?"

"Not...too hard. I have to be careful, though. As you
know, I have this deep-seated Need to Keep Score. And then
to get even if I think I'm losing. And of course you don't
know if you have to get even unless you *do* keep score. I just
wanted to acknowledge that. Say it out loud so I can hear it."

"Always safer to say things out loud," said Tyler.
"Preferably so another person can hear."

"You know why I'm keeping score?"

"...Leverage? You want something in return?"

"I'm amazed at how much of a slug I can still be," I said. "It's embarrassing."

"Of course it is. If it wasn't you probably would have already told me."

"I'm keeping score because...I may want a favor from her in the future and I can use my surrender about the wedding as a bargaining chip."

"Why am I not surprised? Just what kind of favor were you thinking you might want?"

"Oh," I said. "...Just some kind of favor."

"The truth now."

"I should never get started with you, you know that? You just can't leave things alone. That's why they killed Socrates. He just wouldn't leave well enough alone. He had to keep picking at everything."

"What kind of favor was that?"

"You don't have to know everything, Tyler. Doesn't say anywhere that I have to tell you everything."

"No, it doesn't. And we can perhaps revisit the issue later. For now let's just leave it and get on with Tradition Seven."

I jumped right in before he could change his mind:

"...*Every A.A. group ought to be fully self-supporting, declining outside contributions.* You know we say that at every meeting, *We're going to pause now and pass the basket to observe the Seventh Tradition.* But nobody bothers to explain to the newcomers what the Seventh Tradition is. They probably think we're some kind of down-on-our-luck con artists out to fleece them out of what little money they have left after years of reckless drinking."

"They used to ask the newcomers *not* to contribute for just that reason. Some places they'd say, *Take some money out if you need carfare.*"

"That was the old days, Maestro."

"You don't think we could do that now?"

"Not a chance."

"Ye of little faith."

"No, it's Me of great reality."

"You underestimate your brothers and sisters in recovery."

"You remember Robert from the Big Sunday Night meeting over on Exposition? The one in the church basement?"

"Racetrack Robert. Always had the racing form with him."

"Which he used to read *during* the meeting," I said. "Which should have told us something. But the guiding lights, the elders, like you, Maestro, decided that they should make him treasurer so he could learn something about responsibility. All went well for the first few months. Or so they thought. Then they discovered that Robert hadn't been paying the rent. At all. Not once did he pay the rent. He was down at Santa Anita playing the ponies with the rent money; buying hay for those broken-down nags he was so fond of. You remember they finally kicked us out because we were so far in the hole with the rent that we couldn't catch up."

"It's a little unfair to use Robert as an example," said Tyler. "Robert had a serious gambling problem. It'd be like putting Big Jane in charge of the donuts. Risky business."

"Exposition was a big meeting, Maestro. I bet we had two hundred people there some nights. Robert was taking our money and betting on the horses."

"Do I hear some righteous indignation here?"

"Of course, he…"

"As I recall, there was a movement to ban him from meetings."

"There was some talk of that," I admitted.

"I bet you guys forgot to check the rest of the First Tradition:

No A.A. can compel another to do anything; nobody can be punished or expelled.

"…Do we deny him his chance to live sober because he's a thief?"

"This guy was stealing our money, Maestro. Money we use to carry the message. Recovery money."

"You ever steal anything, Edward?"

"Oh, little stuff when I was a kid. Candy. Bubble gum. Some pencils from school one time."

"Well, we're only talking about coffee, donut and rent money. Hardly a tragedy."

"There were hundreds of dollars involved. Maybe thousands."

"So we put a price tag on life?"

"Oh, Tyler…You're so…humanitarian sometimes. He probably took some of your money, too."

"You can always get more money."

"Easy for you to say. You've probably got lots of money. I, on the other hand, am a wage slave waiting for my ship to come in."

"Actually," said Tyler, "I live on Social Security and a small pension. Emphasis on small."

"Even worse. He's stealing from a poor old man on limited income. I'd be incensed. I *am* incensed, for chris-sakes. For you if not for myself."

"We're not getting all of our future members from the Social Register, Edward. Some, yes, but not all. For a variety of reasons, some come to us via the jail route. And they're not all getting well at the same time. Besides, getting well is another one of those moving targets. Who decides what well is?"

"I would think that being responsible is a sign of wellness."

"True, but responsibility comes slowly to some of us. As a matter of fact, to some of us, responsibility will always remain an alien concept."

"Well, what about those guys, Maestro? The guys who never *do* anything; guys that just hang around and drink the coffee."

"What about them?"

"I mean can they just go around being irresponsible, stealing the donut and rent money, and we don't do anything about it?"

"Should we throw them out?" said Tyler. "Perhaps bring charges of some kind? Have a committee that decides who gets in and who doesn't? Or who stays in and who doesn't?"

"...Maybe."

"One of A.A.'s early friends in psychiatry described alcoholics as immature, irresponsible, self-centered and rebellious."

"This guy was a friend?" I said.

"A friend honest enough to tell us what our character defects were."

"I'm not that way."

"...More will be revealed," said Tyler.

"I *was* that way...early on."

"You might want to check with one or two of your ex-wives. The ones you married sober. They often have insights into our character defects we've overlooked."

"Jeez, Tyler...Give me some credit. I've come a long way in the last almost-eleven years."

"...You're right; you have come a long way. My apologies...the criticism was unnecessary."

"You making an amend?" I said.

"I am."

"Accepted," I said, before he could change his mind.

"So," he said. "Tradition Seven."

"This is just like the Sixth Tradition; all about money."

"Actually the Sixth Tradition was about lending the A.A. name to an outside enterprise, like A.A. Cola or Sober Suds, lest problems of money, property, et cetera divert us from our primary purpose."

"You know Sober Suds could also be a laundry detergent," I said. "I just thought of that."

"Brilliant."

"But then, who's wacky enough to care if their clothes got washed with Sober Suds?"

"Nobody," he said.

"Right. Nobody…So why did I even bring it up?"

"I have no idea. Maybe you thought it was an insightful comment. "

"I doubt it," I said. "Sometimes I think I talk just to hear myself talk. Maybe to avoid thinking."

"Now *that* may be an insightful comment."

"Maybe…So A.A. doesn't accept money from anybody? What if a group was broke; could they borrow money from another group?"

"The long form of the Tradition says that…*The A.A. groups ought to be fully supported by voluntary contributions of their own members*. Their own group members."

"There goes my clever borrowing idea."

"I think there's even a limit on how much you can leave A.A. in a will. I don't know how much, but it's not much."

"If I was rich and I wanted to donate a million dollars to A.A., they wouldn't accept it?"

"No," he said. "They figured that a fat treasury might tempt the General Service Office to invent all kinds of things to do with the money. We'd be a rich corporation. Think of all the worthy causes we could support. Imagine A.A. as a rich, philanthropic corporation."

"What's wrong with that? Better than General Motors being rich. At least we'd do something good with the money. GM'd just build another thousand cars that guzzle gas."

"The trustees incorporated an important policy when they decided that A.A. must always stay poor. Bare running expenses plus a prudent reserve is the financial policy."

"So what's a prudent reserve?" I said.

"Traditionally, for the groups anyway, it's a month, maybe two, for rent, coffee and literature."

"I could call our Central Office and find out for sure."

"You could. And if they don't know, you could call the New York Central Office and ask them."

"They'd tell me?"

"They would, but don't be surprised if they throw it back in your lap and say it's an individual group issue—a local issue if you will—and good luck with the resolution."

"Is being self-supporting a spiritual principle?" I said.

"You tell me," said Tyler.

"Why do I even bother asking you questions?"

"If you figure it out yourself, you'll remember it. If I tell you, you'll forget it before the sun comes up."

"Who was the gal who always said, *I have a job and I'm self-supporting through my own contributions?*"

"Ardella," he said.

"Right. How do you forget a name like Ardella?"

"Sweet Lady. So you were about to explain how self-supporting could be a spiritual principle."

"Self-supporting could mean…independent."

"Could be. Why is independence a spiritual principle?"

"Eh…Why is independence a spiritual principle?"

"I just said that."

"I know. I'm thinking about it…"

"I'll wait," he said. "Don't rush."

"There might be different kinds of independence. Maybe …material independence and spiritual independence."

"That's two different kinds."

"In that case…I think it's *material* independence that might qualify as a spiritual principle."

81

"Why?"

"Because," I said, "*spiritual* independence is part of that I-Can-Do-It-Myself syndrome. You know, The Lone Ranger thing where I go off to fight the demons and dragons by myself. I sometimes forget the first rule in sobriety—*My way doesn't work.*"

"That's a little fuzzy, but acceptable on short notice."

"...It's about...sexual favors."

"What's about sexual favors?"

"That's the kind of favors I was thinking about when you asked me what I wanted in return for my surrender. You know, from Sally."

"I see," said Tyler. "So it wasn't really a surrender."

"Of course it was. I surrendered to her desire to have this...stupid big wedding. Gave in. Absolutely a surrender."

"No, surrender is yielding power, control or possession to someone else. You were simply involved in an exchange of goods and services. A trade agreement if you will. There were strings attached. You had this trump card you were going to play at some opportune time. Then you were going to say, *I gave you this and now you have to give me that.* Whatever *that* is. The Barter System."

"Actually, it's not a big deal anyway," I said. "A minor issue at best. The whole thing. And I'd never say you *have* to do this. Or that. That would be like using force. I'd just ask. Politely."

"But not so minor that you felt you didn't have to have some leverage to get it done."

"I probably never would have used it. The leverage."

"But you felt that you needed it."

"Well...She's shown little indication that she'd like to do...this thing I'm thinking about."

"My suggestion?" said Tyler. "You two better start talking be*fore* you get married. How many times have you been through this and you don't know by now that if you don't put all the cards on the table in the beginning, you have no chance of a successful relationship? Zero. None. There's this new thing called communication, where people actually talk to one another, say what they like and don't like, how they feel about certain things. Write it down. Ask questions. The cards that fall out of your sleeve later on are all poison cards, no matter how innocent you think they are."

"I'd like to get back to the Tradition now."

"...It's probably the safer path at the moment. You were saying that spiritual independence might not be the way to go. So where does that leave us with material independence?"

"...Material independence just might be a true spiritual principle. It would mean that our reliance, our dependence if you will, would be on a Higher Power instead of a new sports car or a big-screen teevee. Substance rather than shadow."

"Higher Power instead of General Motors," he said. "HP not GM. Tradition Seven. God or Mammon."

"Exactly. I'm not relying on what's Out There to make me okay. To stamp my ticket. I'm self-supporting...*we're* self-supporting through our own contributions. Financially *and* emotionally."

"What about the Community?" he said.

"What about it?"

"Isn't the Community something that's Out There?"

"...I never think of it that way," I said. "I think of living *in* community. Being a part of it. It's not something I have to get, it's something I am—a member of the Community."

"Good. You know, Bill W said that his basic flaw was his almost absolute dependence on people or circumstances to supply him with prestige and security."

"Bill said that?"

"When he was talking about emotional sobriety. But that's not you. Not now."

"Nope," I said, too quickly as it turned out.

"Because you're already okay. I love it. You realize that life's working from the inside out, the way it's supposed to. So this thing you've got going with Sally, or this thing that you'd like to get going with Sally, isn't really something that you need. Or even want. Because your final reliance is on... on what?"

"...On my Higher Power."

"Well said, Star Pupil."

He seemed positively gleeful. Sometimes I could just kill him when he does things like that and I end up agreeing with some bizarre statement that I don't actually agree with at all. But of course I didn't let on; I didn't want to give him the satisfaction of thinking he'd gotten to me with his devious logic.

"Tradition Eight next week?" I said calmly.

"Tradition Eight it is."

"I want you to know that I'm going to think very carefully about independence and being fully self-supportting."

"That's nice, Edward. A good way to spend the week."

"Actually I'm not at all sure we didn't get sidetracked somewhere in the discussion and I ended up agreeing to something that I really don't agree with."

"That happens sometimes," he said innocently. "Give it some thought. I leave you with an Islamic saying... *Forgetfulness of self is the remembrance of God.*"

"I'll remember that."

"It a good thing to remember."

"Goodnight."

"Goodnight."

TRADITION EIGHT

Alcoholics Anonymous should remain forever non-professional, but our service centers may employ special workers.

The laborer is worthy of his hire.

Luke 10:7

"I thought about what we talked about last week," I said.

"And…?"

"I'm not sure we weren't discussing apples and oranges. How did we ever get from talking about being self-supporting, which is Tradition Seven, to material independence as a spiritual principle, to Sally and me? *And*, Maestro, *and* the implication, don't think I missed it, the implication that I was somehow at fault in requesting certain…things from my soon-to-be bride."

"No fault in requesting. None. But what you give, you need to give freely. Without the strings I see dangling from the gift box. When you give something, or surrender a cherished position, and you have certain considerations attached, you're not giving, you're simply bartering. You're trading things, in this case your approval to have a bigger wedding, for certain sexual considerations not normally included in the deal. That's not a gift you're giving, that's a trade. Only she doesn't know it's a trade. She actually thinks you saw the light, and out of the generosity of your large, though artificial heart, you're letting her do it the way she wants to do it. Because you love her. Because you see it's really a small issue and not worth arguing about."

"What's all that mean?" I said.

"It means you're selfish. No surprise there."

"…I'm not as selfish as I used to be."

"That's good."

"You're probably selfish, too."

"I am," he said. "What does the Big Book say that the root of our problem is?"

"Selfishness…It says that alcoholics are extreme examples of self-will run riot."

"And if you don't get your way?"

"I throw myself on the floor and have a fit."

"That's one option, though the tantrum thing loses its appeal when you get older. Nothing worse than seeing a fifty-year-old having a tantrum. Very unbecoming. Most of us have refined the process and try to get what we want some other way."

"So," I said, "you think I might have leveraged my encounter to get what I wanted at some future date."

"It's obvious, Noble Student. Look, if this favor you want is a deal-breaker, better find out now. Put the last card you have up your sleeve on the table, and play with a full deck."

"She may leave," I said.

"Better now than later. After you buy the house, have that one love child she's always wanted, it's a much tougher deal."

"We're a long way from the Eighth Tradition, Boss."

"I know. Sometimes it can't be helped. Conversations between friends often lead to other topics."

"We should maybe stay focused."

"We shall, though I think your impending nuptials are worthy of a few minutes of dialogue."

"What will the readers think?"

"I don't know. Maybe they'll learn something."

"Tell me that thing you used to say about fear," I said.

"The spiritual path is a journey through the House of Fear. To the extent that I'm willing to take the journey, the greater the peril, the greater the reward."

"Risk all to gain all?"

"Exactly," said Tyler. "The Traditions, as well as the Steps, are all about the application of certain principles—unity, service, love, anonymity, autonomy, freedom, humility, and more…Overlapping principles that guide and direct this society of drunks, this alliance that has been miraculously formed from the clay of human despair."

"So…I should risk everything by telling the truth?"

"That's not really a question, is it?"

"…No. That's a statement. I'll risk everything and tell the truth…But if it backfires, I want you to know that I'm holding you personally responsible."

"This thing is between you and your Higher Power, Edward. And of course Sally. Remember what we talked about—you ask for guidance each morning and leave the house assuming you've received it."

"But how do you know?" I said. "I mean how do you know if you've received it?"

"Easy answer—You don't. That's why they call it Faith. If you knew, they'd call it Fact. How does *I have great Fact in the process* sound?"

"Goofy."

"That's one reason you say things out loud. Preferably so someone else can hear."

"God…"

"To continue, Noble Student…Tradition Eight has been called the Amateur Tradition. You know why?"

"If I remember my first year Latin with Brother Rupert, the word amateur has its root in the Latin *amare*, to love. *Amo, amas, amat—I love, you love, he loves.* Thus, amateur: someone who does something for love rather than money."

"And Brother Rupert thought you were sleeping during class."

"Not a chance."

"Just think of all the new things our readers are learning, Edward. Now it's Latin."

"Don't get too excited, Maestro. As you know there aren't all that many out there. That many readers."

"I know," he said "but they're enthusiastic. Their dedication makes up for the lack of numbers."

"The unfortunate part of all this, Maestro, is that we're never going to get rich and famous unless we get into the Mainstream. The literary Mainstream. This recovery stuff is okay, but we should be thinking courtroom drama, or action/ adventure books. How about a John Grisham knock-off? A kangaroo-court drama set in a dungeon somewhere. I know you could do books like that. Books that sell. A whole new concept for you."

"Perhaps the prison novel will fill the bill."

"I agree, but when do we get started?"

"Patience, Edward. Patience. We have to get through this one first."

"Why? We could skip this one and come back to it later. *After* we're rich and famous."

"It's not about money, Edward."

"Easy for you to say. You don't *need* money. Not like I do. I mean all you spend it on is V8 juice for Mercedes and an occasional midnight horror movie. I, on the other hand, am thinking of getting married and, therefore, will need more. Much more."

"You think they're giving away Viagra these days?"

"…You and Mercedes?" I said.

"Who else?"

"God." I could only shake my head. "How in the world did I ever get hooked up with you?"

"Because you intuitively realized that, among other things, sexuality and spirituality were not mutually exclusive endeavors. That's one reason. As you know, there were others."

I nodded without speaking.

"Anyway," he said, "you're partially famous already. I mean your name *does* appear as the author of the books. Your picture's even on the back of some of them."

"As you know, that's not my real name. And that's not my picture. That's not even *your* picture. If I ever appear in public, I'll have to have plastic surgery."

"Your own face is just fine the way it is, Edward."

"Besides, famous people are rich, Maestro. That's why they go hand in hand—Rich *and* Famous. No use being famous if you can't be rich."

"A great segue back into the Eighth Tradition, which is meant to ensure our nonprofessional status."

"At last. So what does nonprofessional really mean?"

"The long form of the Tradition," said Tyler, "defines professionalism as the occupation of counseling alcoholics for fees or hire."

"Like you couldn't hire out for five dollars a step? Maybe twenty bucks to get through the Fourth and Fifth."

"Definitely not," said Tyler. "A clear violation. The truth of the matter is that most alcoholics don't trust people who get paid to help them. People have been trying to help alcoholics for years. The deeper truth is that very few recoveries have ever been brought about by the world's professionals, whether psychiatric, medical or religious. Turns out that most alcoholics will only listen to other drunks who have no monetary motive."

"We're a suspicious lot, aren't we."

"We are. You know, before there were the Twelve Steps, there were six, what they used to call the Working Program."

"In the Olden Days," I said.

"In a galaxy far, far away."

"That must be my cue...What were the Six Steps, Zen Master?"

"I thought you'd never ask."

"I waited for the cue."

"First," he said, "was *Admitted we were powerless over alcohol etc.,* second, *Got honest with ourselves,* third, *Got honest with another person,* fourth was the amends step, and the fifth was that *We worked with other alcoholics without demand for money or prestige.*"

"What was the sixth?"

"Asked God to help us do these things. But for our purposes, we'll concern ourselves with the Fifth Step, which seems to indicate that there may have been a time when some members charged money for what we now consider Twelfth Step work."

"Definitely a no-no."

"Definitely. *Freely ye have received, freely give,* is what it says in the Twelve and Twelve."

"Sounds biblical," I said.

"Might be. They got lots of stuff out of the Bible. Especially Dr. Bob. And actually, if it wasn't for the people in it, Christianity might not be all that bad."

"You're getting soft, Maestro. I remember a time when you wouldn't even talk about Christianity."

"I know. But even now, when I think of some of those self-righteous..."

"Easy, Boss. You don't want to get your heart going sideways again. Besides, I thought you'd already made your amends."

"I did. But as you know, resentments have a way of creeping back into our lives."

"Maybe you ought to try another letter to the Pope."

"I already did."

"He answer?" I said.

"No. More silence from the Vatican. And while we're on the subject, I don't like the medications I have to take. They make me crazy."

"The meds for your...condition?" I said.

"Yeah. They give me anxiety attacks. I never had an anxiety attack in my life before I started taking those things. Calcium channel blockers, anti-arrhythmics, blood thinners. God..."

"You? Anxiety attacks? Why have I never heard about this?"

"Oh...It's no big thing," said Tyler. "Besides, I don't have to tell you everything."

"That's my line, Maestro...But given the fact that I happen to know that your sponsor is no longer among the living, and that you probably don't have another one yet, the answer is Yes, you do have to tell me everything."

"Ahhhh..."

For a moment, I found myself almost feeling sorry for him. Almost. Fortunately, I didn't say anything. If there's one thing he hates, it's people feeling sorry for him. His comment goes something like...*I did enough self-pity out there drinking. I don't need any more.*

"So," I said. "You got a resentment list started?"

"Ahhhh..."

"You already said that."

He opened his notebook to the last page and wrote something down.

"You know what you always say, Maestro."

"No, what is it I always say?"

"Two things. *I'm as sick as I am secretive,* and, *There's a part of me that speaks, a part that thinks and a part that writes. To get down to Causes and Conditions I need to use all three.*"

"I said that?"

"And not too long ago."

"Huh," he said. "The Viagra must be affecting my memory. So...where were we?"

"The resentment list," I said.

"Before that."

"*Freely ye have received, freely give.*"

"Right...So, when an A.A. member talks for money, whether at a meeting or to a newcomer, it has a bad effect on everyone."

"And this is for why, Maestro?"

"Because the Money Motive compromises everything he says and does."

"So how come we pay people to run Central Office, man the phones, get all that literature sent out. How come we don't just get volunteers?"

"Well, they tried that. Didn't work. But then paying them was a bone of contention, too. All those cooks, caretakers and secretaries were accused of *making money out of A.A.*"

"Couldn't get anyone to work thirty or forty hours a week for free, eh?"

"No," said Tyler. "The idea was not to pay people to *do* Twelfth Step work, it was to pay them so that Twelfth Step work would be *possible*. But in the beginning, they caught a lot of flak. People wouldn't ask them to speak at meetings. They ignored them or treated them like second-class citizens. The ultraconservative among us may have thought that personal redemption could be obtained only if secretaries and the like would be willing to work at some salary well below the minimum wage."

"Maybe we thought they'd be glad to work for free as a sort of atonement for a wasted life."

"A penance perhaps?" said Tyler. "They ought to be glad to work for A.A. at any salary? Lucky we don't put them in chains?"

"Well..."

"Bill said that if the issue wasn't resolved, nobody but a saint or an incompetent could work for us."

"And of course he probably figured out early on that we'd be short on saints and long on incompetents."

"Indeed," said Tyler.

"What about the people who get sober and get jobs in the alcoholism field? You know, counselors, social workers, and the rest who use the stuff they learned in A.A. as part of their job."

"As long as they don't use the name Alcoholics Anonymous, it's okay."

"So I can't say that I'm Edward Bear, a member of Alcoholics Anonymous and a counselor at the Shady Side Recovery House?"

"No."

"Why?"

"Because," said Tyler, "for one thing you're lending the name to an outside facility, namely the Shady Side Recovery House—think Tradition Six. For another, you're breaking your anonymity."

"But as a member of A.A. I could work in the recovery house."

"You could do that. They just didn't want anyone to use the A.A. name to finance some outside venture. They felt that spirituality and money wouldn't mix."

"But you think they would?...Will?"

"What I said was that sexuality and spirituality were not mutually exclusive. Neither are money and spirituality."

"But somewhat dangerous in the same sentence?" I said.

"...Only maybe."

"And how did you come to this conclusion, Maestro? These conclusions."

"Think of Life as a Tapestry, Edward; everything in it is connected by threads that are woven together. Sexuality is one of the threads, as are spirituality, money and lots of other things…You could even think of the threads as yarn, which also brings to mind the storytelling aspect of life in recovery. A good Yarn, so to speak."

"This going to be one of those long, philosophical explanations? If it is, I'm going to take notes. Just in case you ask questions later."

"This won't take long; a small piece of paper will do."

"I've been through this too often to believe that," I said. "I'll use a large piece of paper and write small."

"You know what a loom looks like?"

"Of course I know what a loom looks like, Tyler. You think I'm some kind of a dummy?…Never mind. I withdraw the question."

"Anyway the Tapestry, woven on this giant Loom, is composed of threads and fibers that blend together to form something we call Life."

"On a Loom," I said. "On this great…big…giant… Loom …that's in the sky somewhere?"

I always get the raised eyebrow when he thinks I'm being sarcastic.

"You know the primary colors?" he said.

"Sure. I was married to a kindergarten teacher once."

"A perfect match."

"Not really. After dealing with five-and six-year-olds all day, she came home expecting to find an adult. She mistook being bigger for being mature."

"Sad…So what are the primary colors?"

"Easy," I said. "Red, yellow and blue."

"How do you make green?"

"Easy again. You mix yellow and blue. Hey, maybe the marriage wasn't a complete waste."

"But the yellow and blue are still there, right? Even after you mix them together to make green. You just can't see them anymore."

"I want you to know I'm not writing any of this down yet. I'm looking for clarity here."

"Stay tuned," said Tyler. "You remember Meister Eckhart? *The eye with which you see God is the same eye with which God sees you?*"

"I remember," I said.

"Well, that's it."

"...*What's* it?"

"*That's* it."

"What's *that*?"

"The *that* is the interior union of all things...The *Within of Things*, according to Teilhard de Chardin. Everything exists inside the Mind of the Weaver. Everything. You. Me. Your eye and God's Eye. The yellow, the blue, the green."

"Oh," I said, like I was getting it.

"You see," said Tyler, relentlessly plowing through the wasteland of his disordered mind, "the Great Pumpkin, or the Divine Weaver if you prefer, is weaving this Tapestry in which everything is connected. That's a key point. Since it's all connected, everything that happens alters the Tapestry in some way. Every death. Every birth. Even every thought. Spirituality and sexuality and money all have a part to play. They're not good or bad; they're just part of the Tapestry."

"And the colors? Where do they fit in, Professor? How does mixing yellow and blue to get green fit into this divine plan of yours?"

"Because hidden in the yellow and blue is the possibility of green. If they never mix, you'll never know that. But the green already exists in the mind of the Weaver before you mix the yellow and blue. Plus lots of other colors we can't even see. So do spirituality and sexuality, spirituality and money, and spirituality and everything else. The potential for everything already exists."

"...In the mind of the Weaver."

"Right," said Tyler. "There is nothing inherently bad about money or sex or spirituality or anything else. It's how you use them."

"And the eye with which you see God?"

"Is the same eye with which God sees you."

"I know that part, but what does it really mean?"

"Didn't we just discuss that?" said Tyler.

"Yeah, but I didn't get it."

"It means that whether we realize it or not, whether we like it or not, we're all connected. There is within each of us the imprint of the Divine. The separation we sometimes feel is an illusion. I think it was Einstein who called the feeling of separation *An optical illusion of consciousness.* Rumi weighs in with, *God is nearer to you than yourself.* Christ: *The Kingdom of heaven is within.* Buddha: *Look within, thou are the Buddha.* Krishna: *Brahman is present in every act of service.* The biblical story about God knowing when a sparrow falls from the sky is true because God *is* every sparrow."

"So if a chicken falls out of the sky, God is every chicken, too?"

"Right."

"Chicken dinner is God dinner?"

"…You could say that."

"I'm not saying it, at least not in public. So when it says in the Big Book that *Deep down in every man woman and child is the fundamental idea of God,* it means…what?"

"It means that you do not have a soul, you *are* a soul, that the fundamental activating force in your life is spiritual in nature and that you share that reality with every living creature. Everything and everybody is sacred. As Walt Whitman said, *The hand of the stranger is the Hand of God.*"

"Which throws a whole new light on Twelfth Step work," I said. "The problem is, Maestro, that this line of reasoning inevitably leads me to the conclusion that I'm God. I mean if everybody else can be God, why can't I? Which, in case you haven't noticed, is a very New Age concept."

Tyler closed his eyes for a moment.

"Am I right or what?" I said.

"Next time you feel godlike," said Tyler, "you should try getting the traffic light to turn green as you approach an intersection. That way you can work on your Control issues…Now we turn ever so gently to the concept that you are a participant in a Divine Mystery. You are not the originator, you are just a participant."

"Ah, listen carefully, Readers; he's going to play the Divine Mystery card," I said. "The well-know Escape Clause."

"Remember that words can only take you so far in this search, Struggling Student. We labor under the illusion that words can explain everything. Not so."

"I'm putting my pencil away."

"You, Edward, are a participant in this Mystery. So am I. And so is everybody else. The origin of the strands and fibers that *form* the tapestry is hidden from us. Perhaps in a Divine Closet somewhere in deep space where there's a big ball of Yarn. A Cosmic Story, if you will. *All the world's a stage*, as the Bard said."

"*…And all the men and women merely players…*"

"Truth is, there is much that we don't know. That we can't know. What I do know, what I believe, is that you can't get closer or farther away from the Weaver, and, though you may *feel* a separation, there actually is none. Hence the need to make a daily connection, as in…*What we have is a daily reprieve contingent on the maintenance of our spiritual condition.* Daily, as in every day. Check in. Think of it as the spiritual wing of the Global Positioning System."

"Since I'm part of the Tapestry, Maestro, I could ask the Weaver for…various things."

"You could. You are actually encouraged to do just that...*Ask and you shall receive*, it says in another Book. That includes answers, not just BMW's, which seems to be one of the favorite requests. The Eleventh Step talks about *conscious* contact."

"So money is okay? Sex is okay?"

"Everything's okay. There are no mistakes, only lessons."

"I knew there was a catch," I said.

"As long as there's free will, there are choices and the possibility of making poor choices. Hopefully, as Bill says, a lesson will be learned. Either that or you could opt for the Cow God."

"So what's outside the Tapestry."

"Might be nothing," said Tyler.

"Can't be nothing. I mean there's always got to be something."

"Why?"

"Because...Nothing isn't anything. Isn't there always something?"

"When you try to get into the heart of the Mystery, into the Ball of Yarn, or inside the Jewel of the Lotus, you run out of words. That's where we are now. Words explain a three dimensional reality. That's all. Didn't we talk about that a few Traditions back? A meditation practice may give you answers, but you won't be able to put words to them."

"I'm lost...again."

"Good," said Tyler. "If you're truly lost you have a chance to be found. You know—amazing grace. *I once was lost...*"

"Does your sudden sense of oneness with the Universe, or closeness to the Weaver, have anything to do with your erratic heartbeat and your renewed sense of mortality?"

"Ah, Edward...Where would I be without your doubtful and loving heart?"

"You'd be in serious trouble, Maestro. Someday you'll be grateful I'm around."

"I'm already grateful. You know that…But, enough for this week. Next week we'll tackle Tradition Nine."

"And more adventures of the Weaver?"

"Possibly, Star Pupil. Possibly."

"I need clarity, Maestro."

"No, Edward. You need patience."

TRADITION NINE

A.A., as such, ought never be organized; but we may create service boards or committees directly responsible to those they serve.

There can be no real freedom without the freedom to fail.

Eric Hoffer, The Ordeal of Change

"You know," said Tyler, "when they first formulated the Ninth Tradition, it said that *A.A. should have the least possible organization.*"

"That's us—Disorganized Central."

"But, get this, since then they decided that A.A. should never be organized at all."

"They were probably thinking of the South San Pedro Skid Row meeting. Total chaos. You ever been to that meeting?"

"I have," said Tyler.

"Everybody's drunk."

"Well, not everybody. The people that come to put on the meeting are sober."

"Usually."

"So, usually is okay. Nobody's perfect."

"And everybody talks during the meeting. I mean not just the speaker. Everybody just babbles on talking to themselves or long-lost relatives, or no one in particular. The noise level's incredible."

"I know," said Tyler. "But the funny thing is that people get sober there."

"They do?"

"Every once in a while one of the guys who lives on the Row will ask to chair the meeting. And he'll be sober."

"Amazing," I said.

"It is…So the Ninth Tradition says that we're not organized, which may make us the only large organization in the world that's not organized."

"How about the government?" I said.

"Outside issue. Besides, they're *supposed* to be organized. We're not."

"So how come," I said, "since we have no organization, we're creating service boards and committees that are responsible to others? Aren't they organizations?"

"Those are not boards or committees that direct or govern us; they are entities that serve us. You see, early on they discovered that alcoholics couldn't be dictated to— individually or collectively."

"Meet Mr. and Mrs. Immaturity, the leaders in our community here. *Don't tell me what to do! Who do you think you're talking to?*"

"Defiant, rebellious, self-centered, that's us," said Tyler. "So these committees, instead of dictating policy, or leveling fines for aberrant behavior, merely suggest certain solutions. Gently suggest. They are not empowered to do anything other than that."

"And Central Office?"

"Same thing."

"What makes it work?" I said. "No fees, no dues, no rules. Man…"

"Same as the Steps. Unless the individual A.A. member follows the suggested Twelve Steps, he almost certainly, as it says in the Twelve and Twelve, *signs his own death warrant.* The same applies to the Traditions. Unless the group tries to function within the Traditions, it soon withers and dies. Enough groups die, alcoholics begin to die, because one of the things we have learned along the way is that, *most alcoholics can't survive unless there is a group.* All of which hammers home the importance of the Traditions and the fact that we can't do this alone."

"Still, it's amazing that anyone gets sober," I said. "You see some of those people down on Skid Row?"

"I have, though I might remind you that you weren't exactly a candidate for high office when you stumbled in the door."

"Bad, eh?" I said.

"Somewhere between pathetic and hopeless."

"I still had a car..."

"And a watch, I noticed. A veritable treasure trove of material goods. And I believe you were still married to some unfortunate soul."

"I was," I said.

"And you were ve-ry angry. I remember that. Still, you had the most important ingredient."

"Which was what?"

"Desperation. You looked and acted like somebody who had already come to realize one of the great truths in Recovery: *My way doesn't work.* Add to that a goodly dose of despair and hopelessness and we have someone that alcohol has beaten into a state of reasonableness."

"Reasonableness meaning that I was willing to do anything..."

"...Go to any lengths," he said.

"Right. Go to any lengths to get sober."

"The perfect First Step position; the realization that we are powerless over booze."

"So the alcoholic conforms to the Traditions because ...?"

"First of all," said Tyler, "because we must; our lives depend on it. Second, because we love the kind of life that obedience to them brings. Bill says that, *Great love and great suffering are A.A.'s disciplinarians; we need no others.*"

I flipped open my notebook.

"He also said that... *Our atheists and agnostics widened our gateway, so that all who suffer might pass through, regardless of belief or lack of belief...*"

"Well done," he said. "Wrong Tradition, but I like the quote."

"Wrong Tradition?"

"Probably belongs in Three."

"Oh...I just wanted you to know I was doing my research."

"I'm making a note of it."

"So the service boards or committees don't really govern anything?"

"No," said Tyler.

"Don't you think that's strange?"

"I do. Why do you think they don't give orders or govern anything?"

"Because alcoholics are too immature and rebellious to accept any kind of direction?"

"That's part of it," said Tyler. "That and the fact that these service boards and committees function as transmitters of the invaluable lessons of experience."

"So we don't have to reinvent the wheel time and time again?"

"Right. Besides manning the phones and answering mail, they are also available to share experience, strength and hope about certain issues that come up over and over again."

"Like what?" I said.

"Anonymity issues, singleness of purpose issues, court-ordered people at meetings, the politics of sobriety, the list is long."

"But they don't give advice. Even if you ask for it."

"No. They might suggest a certain pamphlet, or a reading out of some of the other literature, but they are unlikely to tell you what to do. They are more likely to say that the problem has arisen elsewhere and the majority experience seems to suggest…a certain solution."

"A.A. is just full of rebellious souls, isn't it?"

"It is. Radicals, rebels and revolutionaries. People who could not obey-the-rules."

"And it still works."

"It does," he said. "We are bound together by certain principles, spiritual in nature, that make cooperation imperative. We talked about that last week."

"I know. I'm still trying to digest some of last week's ideas. Chicken dinner, God dinner. Man…"

"…*Any man's death diminishes me…*"

"For I am involved in Recovery?"

"True…But then we are led to the larger framework … *For I am involved in Mankind.*"

"What if a guy didn't care about other people?" I said. "About anybody? What if he didn't feel anything about other people dying or being sick or being in pain? Even people close to him."

"A guy like you or me?"

"…Maybe. I mean lots of times I really do try to care, but sometimes I don't seem to have an emotional connection to life. Or to people. I don't seem to feel things that other people feel. I'm not even sure I know what love is. Been married four times and I don't think I have a clue. It scares me. I used to wonder about that when I was young. When everybody else had their eyes closed and were thinking holy thoughts and having pious feelings right after communion,

I was thinking about MaryLou with the great body who was kneeling in the pew in front of me...probably thinking holy thoughts about Jesus."

"And you think you were the only one doing that?" said Tyler.

"I never heard anyone talk about it."

"And of course you never talked about it either."

"You crazy? That'd be like telling somebody you were chewing on the Host after communion. Father Osgood had informed us if we did that it would be like chewing on Jesus. Made you an immediate candidate for Eternal Damnation. So you spent a lot of time trying to get this gummy wafer off the roof of your mouth with your tongue."

"You ever chew it?" said Tyler.

"...I did."

"And...?"

"I expected to get struck by lightning, but nothing happened."

"Were you relieved?"

"No," I said, "Actually I was a little disappointed. I just felt guilty. But then I felt guilty about everything. And I never confessed it. That was the start of my downfall. Well, maybe not the start. But close to the start."

"So in spite of all the rules we had growing up, they didn't keep us from experimenting with other...options?"

"No," I said.

"The Ten Commandments probably would have worked better for drunks if they were suggestions rather than commands."

"Too many *Thou shalt nots?*"

"Definitely," he said. "Thou shalt not steal, commit adultery, bear false witness, et cetera...Those are known as opportunities for alcoholics."

"You think the Ten Suggestions would've worked better?"

"I do," said Tyler. "I see a whole new movie experience about Moses: The Ten Suggestions, starring Harvey Keitel and Robert Duvall."

"Which one's Moses?"

"Keitel," said Tyler.

"And who does Duvall play?"

"As I remember the story, Moses had a brother named Aaron."

"Be a terrible waste of talent to put Duvall in a minor role. He'd be better as Moses. Or God even."

"But just think of all the intensity Keitel could bring to the role," said Tyler. "Can't you see him smashing the Tablets when he gets down off the mountain and sees his people worshiping a golden calf. Graven images, homeboy. False gods."

"You think Budweiser could be a false god?"

"Could be. Was for some of us. How many times have you turned your life and your will over to the makers of Jack Daniels? Or to the barmaid at the Zanzibar?"

"Too often," I said.

"And instead of calling Central Office, which is one of those service boards or committees they refer to in the Ninth Tradition, you were dialing the Zanzibar Club to see if Melody was tending bar."

"I called Central Office one night and got an answering service."

"And they said they'd have somebody call you."

"Right. But I didn't wait. I called the Zanzibar instead of waiting for a callback."

"So you went to the Zanzibar Club," said Tyler.

"I did. But I did wait awhile for somebody to call."

"How long is awhile?"

"Oh...maybe five minutes," I said.

"Five whole minutes?"

"To be honest, it probably wasn't even that long. I probably just hung up and dialed the Zanzibar."

"Because you wanted to drink."

"I did," I said. "But when I was really ready to quit. I called Central Office and you, of all people, showed up."

"I'd been waiting for you to get ready."

"So when I called, you knew?"

"I knew," said Tyler.

"You knew before that?"

"...Yeah."

"How?"

"Oh...some things are just known."

"Is this part of the Tapestry story?" I said. "The everything-is-connected scenario? You were just a couple of threads away waiting for me to call?"

"Part of a good Yarn, so to speak," he said. "You ever wonder what would have happened if there hadn't been anyone at Central Office to answer the phone that day?"

"...Maybe I never would have made it. Maybe that opportunity never presents itself again and I go spiraling into the tank."

"A possibility...But we'll leave that discussion for another night. On to next week and the Tenth Tradition. *A.A. has no opinion on outside issues...*"

"And almost everything is an outside issue."

"Just about," he said. "You might want to think about talking to Sally this week."

"That's just a suggestion, right?"

"Of course."

"Because we don't tell each other what to do."

"Right," he said. "We suggest possible solutions. We share what happened to us when we tried to do something really insane. Like you're doing."

"So that, hopefully, the recipient of this…guidance will listen and benefit from your experience, strength and hope. Does it ever work that way?"

"Rarely. Usually what happens is that the newcomer does this really insane thing anyway and learns from his or her own experience. If he survives it. Which means, among other things, that he will be more likely to remember it. And we hope that it isn't necessary for him to drink after such a disastrous, ill-advised episode."

"But you don't tell him, *I told you so.*"

"We try very hard not be judgmental, though we do not always succeed. It is almost too tempting at times to gloat about how smart we think we are. But everyone has his or her own path. Do the Steps, honor the Traditions, walk out the door and live life."

"Simple but not easy?"

"Simple but not easy. So, as a suggestion, put all the cards on the table and play it straight up with Sally. You might be surprised."

"I'm not sure I know how to play with all the cards on the table," I said.

"Never too late to learn, Noble Student."

TRADITION TEN

Alcoholics Anonymous has no opinion on outside issues; hence the A.A. name ought never be drawn into public controversy.

Wanting to reform the world...is like trying to cover the whole world with leather to avoid the pain of walking on stones and thorns. It is much simpler to wear shoes.

Ramana Maharshi

"You seem especially cheerful tonight," said Tyler. "Did life treat you well last week?"

"It did. And you were right, though I sometimes hate to admit it. I don't think it's good for your humility."

"What was I right about?"

"You remember what we talked about last week?"

"Ah, Sally. You must be referring to that ace of clubs you had hidden up your sleeve."

"That's it."

"Don't tell me you put all the cards on the table, shuffled them, and played the hand you got?"

"I did," I said.

"The age of miracles is still with us."

"And you know all that worrying I did about...that certain thing?"

"The sexual thing...Which was what?"

"I can't go into it. I mean not in the book we're doing. This is a family book, right?"

"It started out that way."

"Well, we can't put stuff like that in a family book, Tyler. We want it to be wholesome."

"There's nothing unwholesome about sex, Noble Student. It's basically how we all got here."

"I know that, but this...certain thing doesn't belong in the book."

"Then I bow to your greater wisdom."

"It's not so much about wisdom, Maestro. It's more about...sensibilities."

"Ah, sensibilities. One of my worst character defects; my insensitivity. And you think we'd offend our readers?"

"We might. Why take a chance?"

"Why indeed," he said. "So you suggested this depraved practice to your intended and she...what? Fainted? Called the police?"

"First of all, it's not depraved. It's just...different. She said...she said she'd love to do it. Can you believe it?"

"Another miracle. Demonstrating once again an ancient truth: if you want something it's best to ask for it. Take action. For years I followed the time-honored method of thinking you could guess what I wanted...then getting angry when you couldn't. It's very biblical...*Ask and you shall receive... Knock and it shall be opened...*"

"That may be something of a misrepresentation, Maestro. Isn't that about asking God for things?"

"We are merely suggesting a broader application of a spiritual directive."

"Oh."

"You realize, of course, that our faithful readers are now eagerly waiting for you to divulge this secret desire."

"Can't," I said. "Maybe in the prison book we can tell them."

"No, it's probably better to let them just imagine what it is. That's what I'm doing. But enough of these outside issues. On to Tradition Ten."

"I don't view my personal life in recovery as an outside issue."

He hesitated for a moment; a sure sign that he was thinking about what I had said.

"Well..."

"How's the resentment inventory coming?" I said, pushing my luck.

"...Okay."

"You're actually doing it? I mean you've started writing?"

"I've got some things down." He sounded defensive. Which I took as a good sign.

"You going to have it ready soon?"

"...Why are you badgering me? I feel like I'm on trial."

"I'm not badgering you, Boss. I'm merely reminding you that you said you were going to do some inventory work on a few resentments that had crept up over the past year or so, and I was just wondering...like when you were going to have it done."

"I don't remember doing this to you."

"You don't? How about the time I was doing my first fourth step? Remember you were on my case like I couldn't believe. Every time I saw you, you wanted to know if I was finished."

"That was different," said Tyler. "You were new and you took six months to get it done. Six months. I was afraid we might lose you if you didn't finish it soon."

"There was a lot of sordid stuff on my first inventory."

"And on some of the others, too," he said.

I tried to look hurt, but I should have known that that never works with him.

"Okay," I said. "You win. I..."

"It's not about winning, Edward. You know that. And I'll have it done before we finish the Traditions."

"Promise?"

"...I'll have it done," he said. "Now tell me what you know about the Tenth Tradition."

"I read up on it in the Twelve and Twelve...And The Language of the Heart."

"Commendable."

"The Tenth Tradition reminds us that we must never publicly take sides in a fight."

"What about the worthy causes?"

"No way," I said.

"Not even Politics, AIDS, Gun Control, Abortion, Terrorism, the really important issues of the day?"

"Nope."

"How so, Noble Student?" said Tyler. "Surely our society is entitled to comment on the issues confronting us in these troubled times."

"Because Obi-Wan, when the Traditions were written, our founders felt that controversy might actually endanger Alcoholics Anonymous itself. And since their lives depended on the survival of the community, the small effect they could have on public policy would hardly be worth the risk."

"Well done, Edward. And you remember what we said about the Washingtonians."

"About their demise as a society?"

"Yes."

"For one thing," I said, "they got heavily involved in the social issues of the day. They allowed speakers of all kinds, alcoholics *and* nonalcoholics, to use the Washingtonian platform to further causes like Prohibition, the abolition of slavery and a raft of outside issues."

"And when they tried to reform America's drinking habits they were headed for doomsday. But the lessons were not lost on our founders. What does the Fifth Tradition tell us?"

"*Each group has but one primary purpose...*"

"And the Preamble?"

"Eh...*Our primary purpose is to stay sober and help other alcoholics to achieve sobriety...*Bet you didn't think I knew that."

"As always, I'm impressed by the breadth of your knowledge. What's the sentence before that?"

"...Before *Our primary purpose...*?

"Yeah," said Tyler "...The one before that."

"*A.A. is not allied with any sect....* That one?"

"That's the one."

"*A.A. is not allied with any sect, denomination, politics, organization or institution; does not wish to engage in any controversy, neither endorses nor opposes any causes...* How about *that*?"

"Outstanding. I may have to reevaluate your grade for the course. How did you manage?"

"Actually I didn't know I knew it. But after listening to it three or four times a week for almost eleven years, it must have become imbedded in my gray matter."

"Not only that, but available for recall. That's the amazing part. I seem to have trouble remembering anything lately."

"Here's the solution I got from Irv," I said. "You remember Irv?"

"Who could forget Irv?" said Tyler.

"His solution was to write everything down."

"That's why I have this notebook."

"But you don't take it everywhere. It's too big. Irv had a small notebook that fit in his shirt pocket. He thought of something, out came the notebook. He knew if he didn't write it down right away, he'd forget."

"Irv was old, eh? Eighty-something when he died?"

"Eighty-six," I said. "Died on his way to the Friday night Rodeo meeting. With a newcomer of course. Young Harry R, who fortunately happened to be driving."

"I don't forget everything," said Tyler. "Just some things."

"Bet you don't forget to take your Viagra."

"…No. How could I forget something like that?"

"But you probably forget to take your vitamins in the morning."

"Sometimes," he said.

"See, it's a matter of priorities. You have a better chance of remembering the things that are important to you. So the Viagra turns out to be more important than your overall health…Which is just a comment, not a criticism."

"Mercedes reminds me."

"About…?

"The vitamins."

"Oh. She…sleeps over?"

"On occasion. Usually between the full moon and the last quarter."

"I have other questions, Maestro, which I'll save for later. I'll wait till after we finish the Traditions…and you finish your list."

"Write them down so you don't forget."

"I'll do that," I said.

"Returning to the task at hand…You notice that you hear very little talk at the meetings about religion, or medications, or politics, or the government. Occasionally someone will bring up the dreaded medication/anti-depressant topic and people will have to weigh in with various opinions and justifications, pro and con, which only confuses the issue."

"You have an opinion, Maestro?"

"I do. I think if you need to take medication, you should take it. It's a very personal decision. Not being a doctor, I am hardly qualified to advise you on whether you should take medication or not. Somewhere in the Big Book it says, *God has abundantly supplied the world with fine doctors, psychologists…*and so forth. *Do not hesitate to take your health problems to them.*"

"It's an outside issue?"

"I'm not sure," he said. "What I do know is that it seems to generate a lot of controversy, and the meetings often tailspin into justifications, rebuttals and advice-giving. There are those who are perhaps overly impressed with their own abstinence from all forms of medication."

"I heard a guy at a meeting one night say that he'd been sober for fourteen years and he'd never taken so much as an aspirin. Does that mean he's more sober than the rest of us?"

"That's probably what he thinks," said Tyler. "Here's a worse story. Not too long ago, I heard a guy relate how he'd been sitting at a table at York Street a few days earlier talking about the fact that he had to take medication for his *grand mal* seizures. One of our many unlicensed York Street Physicians sitting there told him that he wasn't really sober if he was taking medication. So of course, being new and wanting to do things right, he stopped taking his medication, had a seizure and almost died."

"Dangerous business," I said. "You take anything beside the stuff for your erratic heartbeat?"

"No, but if I had to take other meds, I'd take them… after I got a second opinion. There are lots of doctors in recovery who will help. Dr. Paul said that if medication is recommended, go through the Steps one more time, and if that doesn't help, take the medication."

"Makes sense."

"Basically," said Tyler, "the point they're trying to make is that if we don't make a habit of arguing these problems privately, there's little chance that we'll do it publicly. So, at least at most meetings, you won't find topics like government policy, abortion, medication or other outside issues."

"But we're not all that laid-back, are we? I mean don't we fight and disagree about lots of things?"

"We do," he said. "But we don't publicly make policy statements about anything. A.A. doesn't. We don't support any political candidate, any political position, any piece of legislation no matter how friendly."

"But as individuals?"

"As individuals we don't abdicate our responsibilities. We are, after all, citizens who have certain obligations and responsibilities."

"You vote, Maestro?"

"I do. But I didn't till I was fifty. Sober fifteen years before I voted."

"Why then?"

"I was sleeping with a political activist who absolutely insisted that I vote …Or else…"

"Or else what?"

"Or else she wouldn't sleep with me," said Tyler.

"Was that the sex for citizenship trade?"

"You remember Lysistrata? The Greek play?"

"Aristophanes?" I ventured.

"I think it was Aristophanes. During the Peloponnesian War, Lysistrata persuaded the Athenian wives to withhold their…favors until peace was concluded."

"If this weren't a family-oriented book, I'd say something about that. Much to my credit, I'll refrain…But as I remember it, the strategy worked."

"It did. She even dictated the terms of the peace."

"What we won't do for sex. But you continued to vote after your political activist left."

"I did," he said. "Even after she threw me over for a rabid, tree-hugging environmentalist."

"So you like voting now?"

"I love it," he said.

"Why?"

"I think it's because slowly but surely through the years I have joined or maybe rejoined the human race. For a lot of years I just hung around the periphery, drank and made fun of the participants. I am a part of this thing now, part of Life, part of the Dance. Voting is participating. I can now legitimately criticize all the political people I don't like because I'm willing to vote."

"I don't vote," I said. "And I criticize the government all the time."

"I know that, Edward. And believe me, you'll feel better about it after you vote."

"Voting is an outside issue," I said.

"It is. That's why A.A. has no opinion about it."

"But you do."

"You know me. I have an opinion about everything. Next week we'll discuss the Tradition that deals with our public policy of attraction rather than promotion."

"That's tricky, eh? I mean you don't want to be so anonymous that nobody ever hears about you, but you also don't want to be in the advertising business either."

"We shall carefully walk the tightrope, Noble Student. We'll try to find a Middle Way next week. After all, Buddha did."

"Buddha was probably a lot smarter than we are."

"We'll suit up and show up and see what happens."

"Agreed."

TRADITION ELEVEN

Our public relations policy is based on attraction rather than promotion; we need always maintain personal anonymity at the level of press, radio, and films.

If every A.A. felt free to publish his own name, picture and story, we would soon be launched upon a vast orgy of personal publicity.

Bill W Letter (1949)

"You ever think maybe we're violating the Eleventh Tradition by doing this—writing these books?"

"I have thought about that," said Tyler. "Even went down and got the anonymity pamphlet and read it."

"And your conclusion, Maestro?"

"My conclusion is that no, we're not violating the Tradition."

"Why not?" I said.

"Because we're not claiming membership in any particular fellowship and, most Noble Student, as an additional safeguard, we're not using real names or a real, identifiable picture."

"Who is the guy in the picture?"

"Dan…A good friend from over on the East side."

"Dan the car guy?"

"That's him."

"I don't remember his hair being gray."

"The gray hair's a recent addition," said Tyler. "Just since he started going through the divorce."

"That'll do it."

"Ah, the thrill of marriage."

"And the agony of divorce," I said.

"Certainly something we're both familiar with."

"Four marriages—four divorces. There's a certain symmetry to it."

"That puts you in the professional ranks. I've managed to retain my amateur standing."

"With three divorces?"

"But I'm seventy and you're fifty. So factoring in the legal marrying age, you're getting married and divorced about once every...eight years. Whereas I, being much more stable, am getting married and divorced about every... sixteen years."

"And that means you retain your amateur standing?"

"It does," said Tyler. "Anything over ten years per marriage is considered a success. Thereby ensuring a retention of my amateur standing."

"Is that average time per marriage? Because I know you had one marriage that lasted about ten minutes."

"A little longer than ten minutes," he said. "But it's true we were not well matched."

"Maybe you've lost your amateur standing after all."

"Not as long as I'm keeping score."

"Figures," I said. "I'm sure I don't have to remind you that the Need to Keep Score is one of the Seven Deadly Needs."

"I'm considering it a minor violation. Very minor. Hardly a blip on the screen."

"How do we tie all this in with the Eleventh Tradition?" I said.

"Simple—attraction rather than promotion," said Tyler. "We can start with Irma Parkenwood, my first wife. She was promoting certain…assets."

"What's the difference between attraction and promotion?"

"The dictionary informs us, or at least implies, that one is more active than the other. Attraction is something that… attracts us."

"Not supposed to use the same word in the definition, Boss."

"God…You writers. I'll do it by example. A magnet attracts just by being what it is."

"Even an ugly magnet?"

"Even an ugly magnet," said Tyler. "Things like iron filings are drawn to it. The magnet doesn't have to do anything but be itself, be a magnet, to attract certain things."

"Like iron filings."

"And refrigerator doors."

"Tyler…"

"Promotion, on the other hand, is a more active process. To promote something is to actively support it, to publicize and sell it."

"And we're not selling Alcoholics Anonymous," I said.

"Not as a rule, though occasionally somebody pops up with an idea that could be considered promotional in the worst possible sense."

"Don't I remember seeing ads in the Yellow Pages, something to the effect that if you have a problem with alcohol, here's a number to call?"

"Those are mostly detox centers or residential treatment programs," said Tyler. "The long form of the Tradition says that *A.A. ought to avoid sensational advertising.*"

"But A.A.'s number's in the phone book."

"Hardly sensational. We don't want to be so anonymous that nobody can find us."

"Isn't that promotion? Advertising?"

"No, promoting and advertising is what Irma did when she wore those sweaters that were several sizes too small."

"Irma? Was she your ten minute marriage?"

"Irma Clarise Parkenwood," said Tyler, "The Queen of the Hop. And actually the marriage lasted nearly a year. Ten months and twenty-eight days, to be exact."

"Must've been a long time ago, Maestro. Nobody's named Irma anymore. It's like Maude. The last Maude probably died thirty years ago. And didn't sweater girls go out of style sometime during World War II?"

"A few years after. Now if Irma had merely wanted to attract men, she would have dressed a little more…modestly. There would have been no need for the promotional sweaters and tight skirts."

"Women wore tight skirts in those days?" I said.

"Occasionally," he said. "You think they all dressed in aprons and gingham pinafores?"

"…What are pinafores?"

"Never mind. It's too difficult to explain. You had to be there. The point we're trying to make, that the Tradition is trying to make, is that there's a difference between attraction and promotion, and that we endorse the former and eschew the latter."

"Eschew…I like that word. It means avoid?"

"It does. And feel free to use it with my blessing," said Tyler.

"The second part of the Tradition puts a different spin on it."

"It does," said Tyler. "And this may be the most important part—personal anonymity. The first part warns about the dangers of advertising, boosterism, the flag-waving province of the self-promoter. The second part is about the importance of personal anonymity. The Washingtonians advertised the movement as a…*never failing remedy in all stages of the disease*. Then went on to name various individuals who had recovered. *Here we have Joe Blow, former Drunkard, now completely restored as a useful, tax-paying member of society.*"

"Not a good thing," I said.

"No. Never-failing is not a good way to describe a program dealing with drunks. Though statistics are all over the board and unreliable at best, estimates run from a ten to thirty percent success ratio."

"Meaning what?"

"Meaning that somewhere between ten and thirty percent of alcoholics who are exposed to the recovery process stay sober more than five years."

"But nobody really knows, do they?"

"No…Guesswork at best. What we do know is that the self-promotion as employed by the Washingtonians was not a wise public policy."

"Especially," I said, "when the speakers, lecturers, and other highly visible members of the society got drunk."

"There goes the *never-failing* part of your advertising campaign."

"But if we don't advertise, who does? I mean how do people find out about A.A.? Certainly not from one-line entries in the yellow pages."

"Of course now, since A.A. is pretty well known, there's little need for that. In the beginning it was the newspapers, magazines, the radio, the clergy, who recognized the value of A.A. and carried the message for us."

"I hear we always got good press."

"Nearly always," said Tyler. "I think they liked us because we were actually trying to *avoid* publicity. Something new and unheard of. We made announcements before conventions and gatherings that we weren't to be identified by full name or picture. Still do. We didn't have our hand out for something. We weren't feeding at the public trough. Now *that* was news worth reporting."

"So our friends in the media provided favorable publicity for Alcoholics Anonymous?"

"They did. At first they couldn't understand our insistence on personal anonymity. Then they got it. Here was a society who wished to publicize its principles but not its individual members. As a matter of fact, many in the press got it before our own members did."

"How so?"

"There was a time," said Tyler, "when some of our members thought this anonymity principle was old hat. They were sure that they could expand the fellowship at a much faster rate if they utilized the fame and power of our more recognizable members. *Joe Blow's a member, and he's rich and famous, so this A and A thing must be a good deal.*"

"Until, of course, Joseph Blow ends up with his mug shot on the front page after being arrested for drunk and disorderly."

"Another Star bites the dust," said Tyler. "And out the window goes the small amount of public trust we had managed to garner from using Joe's fame and popularity."

"And our critics would have a field day."

"Which they did. So the General Service Office wrote letters to every news outlet in North America, explaining our anonymity policy and asking their help in guarding what we considered one of our greatest protections—the personal anonymity of A.A. members."

"I assume it worked," I said.

"Mostly. Newspapers sometimes deleted names and pictures of overly zealous A.A. members and frequently reminded them of the anonymity policy."

"I don't think that would happen today, Boss. I think it's anything-for-a-good-story now. The more sensational, the better. Joe Blow's name and picture and his affiliation with the A and A thing would be plastered all over the front page of the Daily Fishwrap."

"Maybe...You should perhaps be grateful they didn't have cameras in elevators in the days when you were making ...a public display of yourself."

"And you know," I said, "what's even more embarrassing is that I remember doing it. More than once, too. It's mortifying. Sad to say, I wasn't always in a blackout. Talk about a showstopper. Somewhere between the third and fourth floor of an unknown hotel, yours truly begins to take a whiz in the corner of the elevator. Casually, like this might well have been an everyday occurrence. *Pardon me, I think I'll take a leak in your elevator now.* I mean people are screaming and yelling, pummeling me with purses. *Stop! Stop!* The next floor everybody gets off the elevator. Everybody. Intuitively understanding that this behavior might well jeopardize my freedom, I get off at the next floor and make a hasty exit via the stairway."

"Smart," he said. "Indecent exposure is not a good thing to have on your rap sheet. People ask embarrassing questions like, *Why in the world would you do such a thing,* and you are left with some lame excuse like, *I don't remember,* which is mostly a lie and not valid anyway, or *Somebody must have slipped me a Mickey.* Not everyone understands alcoholic behavior."

"What's a Mickey?"

"God, the younger generation," said Tyler. "You never heard of a Mickey Finn?"

"Oh...A Mickey Finn. Sure. That's how they used to Shanghai sailors in the olden days. The days of yore. When the ships were wood and the men were iron."

"Among other things. So you could tell them somebody slipped you a Mickey and you ended up in the elevator doing this...deplorable thing."

"Which of course nobody would believe," I said.

"Nobody."

"So would the Elevator Episode be attraction or promotion?"

"Neither. And of course if you get caught, your personal anonymity goes down the tubes, too."

"My name up in lights."

"Just what you need," said Tyler. "Publicity. The Fame Game. But let us close this discussion, which is getting way off track, with a notion put forth in the Twelve and Twelve …*Moved by the spirit of anonymity, we try to give up our natural desires for personal distinction as A.A. members, both among fellow alcoholics and before the general public.*"

"Amen, Maestro."

"Next week Tradition Twelve, more about anonymity."

"I'll be ready. I'll finish with a brilliant burst of… something."

"A brilliant burst of something may be just what you need. Perhaps what *we* need."

"Then we can start on the prison book?"

"As soon as you get this one typed up and off to the printer."

"I'll hurry," I said. "You going to put your real name in the prison book?"

"I haven't decided."

"Just think of all your fans, how disillusioned they'll be if they find out that Tyler, the anonymous mentor in several books that might be considered spiritual, is just another slug with a police record."

"They might find it inspirational," said Tyler.

"I doubt that."

"How would you know? We haven't even started it yet."

"Inspirational is not a word that comes to mind when we talk about the prison book."

"Anyway, it's a work of fiction," he said.

"Yeah, but everybody will think all that stuff happened to you."

"To Tyler…"

"Yeah."

"That's why I'm going to call the main character Smith," said Tyler. "In the prison book. Stanley Smith. What could be more anonymous?"

"Instead of Tyler."

"Yeah."

"…Why?"

"So readers won't associate the main character with Tyler."

"Oh…"

"Anyway," he said, "it'll have your name as the author. Just think of the doors it might open for you."

"*These* books have my name as the author. What good has that done me? Have you checked sales lately, Maestro? These things are not flying out the door like something by John Grisham. Worse yet, as soon as we begin to make a profit, you start giving them away. You have to start developing some business sense."

"Though our fan base may be small, they're extremely loyal."

"Not so loyal they're going to buy ten or twenty books each."

"You never know," said Tyler. "It may go national. Think of all the ex-convicts there are. Thousands. Maybe millions."

"Who most likely don't have enough money to buy even one book."

"You're so…pessimistic."

"Realistic, Boss…Let's finish this conversation next week. I'm beginning to get a headache."

"Which may be because you think too much."

"The esteemed author, Edward Bear, has no comment on the preceding statement...Goodnight, Maestro. Say hello to Mercedes."

"Consider it done."

TRADITION TWELVE

Anonymity is the spiritual foundation of all our traditions, ever reminding us to place principles before personalities.

Expedients are for the hour, but principles are for the ages.

Henry Ward Beecher
Proverbs from the Plymouth Pulpit

"Last Tradition, Maestro."

"So it is."

"You ever get bummed out when we're about to finish a book?"

"Sometimes," he said. "When we're doing it, writing it, I've got that sense of purpose, that I'm-okay-because-I'm-doing-something-worthwhile thing. When it's over…a little of the air tends to go out of the balloon."

"That's the variation of the I-am-what-I-do theme we talked about one time?"

"It is," said Tyler.

"And it never goes away?"

"Let's say it diminishes in intensity. The tremendous sense of urgency begins to fade and you gradually begin to realize that in some way not easy to define, you belong…on the planet, in Recovery, in the Community, whether you're writing a book, performing brain surgery on orphans, or just fishing in some mountain stream. *Be Where You Are* is the suggestion I got. You stand on Holy Ground."

"Doesn't feel all that holy."

"It will," he said.

"When?"

"…When you realize that it's Holy Ground."

"So if I decide that it's Holy Ground, that makes it holy?"

"It's been holy all along. You just didn't realize it," he said.

"…I don't get it."

"It's possible you may not be getting it because you're too busy regretting past failures or waiting for some future … golden opportunity that may, or may not, come to pass. Let's say it's some…event that you're sure will stamp your ticket and make you Okay, capital O. That's called Conditional Reality, the worst possible design for living you could have. It will occur to you someday that you stand on Holy Ground because *who* you are, *what* you are, has sanctified it. You are a Child of the Universe and, as such, loved."

"Can we have another a-men?"

"And you can stop waiting to Get Better because there is no better to get. When you realize that, you will understand that you are living in the moment, hence living in the Hand of God. That awareness may come tomorrow or fifty years from now. It doesn't matter."

"It matters, Maestro. Believe me, it matters."

"Trust me, Noble Student. The day will come when it won't matter."

"Eventually?"

"Eventually. And when that day comes, you will realize, or perhaps remember, that you can just Be, without all the qualifiers—as in Be Smart, Be Rich, Be Successful, Be Admired."

"God…But *you* forget sometimes, too."

"I do. That's one reason I continue to go to meetings—so I can be reminded of who I really am. But enough for now...So what can you tell me about Tradition Twelve?"

"The day will come, Maestro, when I'll explain it to you. But not today. And maybe not tomorrow. But someday."

"Eventually?" he said.

"Just the word I was looking for."

"For the moment," he said. "Let's pretend that eventually is now. Use your imagination."

"...Isn't that cheating?"

"I believe it was Einstein who said, *Imagination is more important than knowledge.*"

"I remember. You said that in *The Dark Night of Recovery.*"

"Strange as it may seem," said Tyler, "there may be people who haven't read *Dark Night.* Besides, it's worth repeating."

"Okay, I surrender...for now. Keep in mind that my surrender may be only temporary."

"I'm making a note of it. Another note."

"And I know what it says, what the Twelfth Tradition says, but I'm not sure I understand why anonymity should be the spiritual foundation of all our traditions."

"It doesn't say *all* of our traditions."

"...It doesn't?"

"No. It just says, *our* traditions."

"I'm sure it says *all* in my book," I said. "Everybody says *all* our traditions"

"I know," said Tyler. "But they're wrong."

"Let me see your Twelve and Twelve."

He slid it across the table and I opened it to the Twelfth Tradition.

"...I'll be damned," I said. "I could have sworn it said all. The Big Book doesn't say all either?"

"No...You remember what happened when we did the Twelfth Step in *The Dark Night of Recovery*?"

"You mean the thing about *Having had a spiritual awakening as a result of these steps, instead of as* the *result of these steps*?"

"Remember how much flak we got via email?" said Tyler. "Some members of the Community could hardly wait to point out the error of our ways. Now you wouldn't think people would notice something like that, but an alarming number did."

"Just goes to show you," I said, "how observant our small but loyal following is."

"But as you know it's still in there—the error. I'm waiting for the second printing so I can change it. Which can only happen if we sell out the first printing."

"That puts the problem right back on the Community; if they were buying more books we'd already have a second printing."

"Should we pray for greater sales, Brother Edward?"

"Seems a bit too...self-serving. Even for us."

"Perhaps," said Tyler. "Anyway, anonymity is the spiritual foundation of our traditions because...?"

"Don't you think *all* is implied in the statement."

"I *do* think so, Edward, but that's not what it says. It just says *our* traditions..."

"You know, Maestro, I'm going to do some research on this. I'm positive my Big Book and Twelve and Twelve say *all*. I mean I just got through reading it. How could I be wrong?"

"...Oh, let me count the ways."

"I'll go so far as to wager a dinner that I'm right and you're...not." I couldn't bring myself to say *wrong*.

"Deal," he said. "You take me to some upscale spot like Diamond Jim's?"

"Anywhere you'd like to go. You can even bring Mercedes."

"I'll start out with *escargot* and then order the most expensive thing on the menu."

"You told me you hate snails."

"For you I'll make an exception."

"So if my Big Book and my Twelve and Twelve say *all*, I'll win?"

"You will. And I'll take you anywhere you want to go."

"The Triangle Club?"

"That's a strip joint, Edward."

"I know, but they serve food, too."

"You mind if I bring Mercedes?"

"You don't think she'd be...offended? I mean by the strippers?"

"No...Mercedes likes women," said Tyler.

"So let me get this straight. You're seventy-something years old and you're dating a bisexual vampire?"

"Edward..."

"You think we should put that in the book?"

"Maybe...We can discuss it later, when you do your final editing."

"Okay."

"So anonymity, Noble Student, is the spiritual foundation of our traditions because they, the Founders, equated anonymity with humility and self-sacrifice. The common good if you will. The Tradition says, as you must know because I'm sure you studied it as part of your assignment... You did read it, didn't you?"

"Of course."

His tone of voice said he didn't believe me, but actually I did read it. Even wrote down some comments.

"...It says that since the Traditions ask that we give up personal desires for the common good, we realize that anonymity—read humility—is the foundation of them all."

"See, it does say *all*," I said. "I knew I read it someplace."
"The commentary says all, not the Tradition itself. It's
not advisable to start changing the wording and syntax to
reflect your interpretation of what they really meant."
"I'm helping."
"Don't. That's how the Bible got so screwed up. People
kept translating and interpreting and throwing out parts they
didn't like until nobody really knows what happened or what
was said. Or who said it."
"I'll try to restrain myself."
"I know our readers will appreciate it…So having estab-
lished that the principle of anonymity is really humility in
action, we are left to define humility…That's your cue."
"…To do what?" I said.
"To define humility."
I checked my notebook. I had him this time.
"Humility is…Unpretentiousness, reserve, restraint,
freedom from pride or arrogance."
"Good, that's…"
"Wait, I'm not finished…Unpresumptuousness, subjec-
tion, resignation, abasement, tolerance, forbearance…"
"Okay, okay," said Tyler. "I got it."
"I just wanted you to know I was doing my homework."
"I'm impressed. Somewhat impressed anyway. Anything
else?"
"This from the Tao…*Humility is the root from which
greatness springs…*"
"…Adequate," said Tyler.
"I tried Winnie-the-Pooh, but he doesn't seem to have
been a very humble bear."
"No?"
"You remember in the beginning of the book when
he told Christopher Robin that he'd like some other name
besides Edward Bear? Some exciting name, I think he said."

"I do," said Tyler. "And Christopher named him Winnie-the-Pooh."

"Right. Then, the narrator asked him what kind of stories Pooh liked and Christopher said that he mostly liked stories about himself because he was *that kind of bear.*"

"Obviously not humility material. So skip Pooh. Which brings us to principles before personalities. And the principles are…?"

"Simple," I said. "I wrote them down when you said them—unity, service, love, anonymity, autonomy, freedom, humility…and more. Or others, I think you said. "

"And the personalities?"

"Are just personalities—people. Principles first, personalities second. If you get personalities first, you may have something resembling a cult."

"What does that say about Christianity?" said Tyler.

"…Let's not go there, Maestro. It's late, we're on the last Tradition and I want to save some time so you can tell me, and our eager readers, about those resentments you've been harboring."

"…Did I say I'd do that?"

"You did. And don't plead memory loss. I know you better than that. Let me feed you some of the suggestions you've given me over the years…*I'm as sick as I am secretive…Share it or wear it…Life works from the inside out… The more I rely on my Higher Power, the more reliable It becomes…*"

"I said all those things?" he said.

"More than once."

"Sometimes…sometimes it's that old thing about, *If enough people think I'm okay, I must be okay.* We ever talk about that?"

"We have."

"I fall back into that when a certain kind of fear reemerges in my life. And then it becomes ve-ry important that everyone think I'm okay. So I don't talk about what's bothering me. I become Always Okay. Superman—bullets and bad feelings bounce right off. I think, *Hey, I've been sober thirty-five years, I ought to be able to handle this.*"

"Secrets?"

"Not big dark secrets, but the little things that I don't want to share because I'm afraid they'll make me look bad."

"Like what?" Don't think I was going to let him off easy just because he's my sponsor.

"Envy, self-pity, pride, arrogance, an unwillingness to accept life on life's terms."

"Examples are requested," I said. He didn't give me The Look, so I figured I was on safe ground.

"Like the medications I take. I told the Doc, *Hey, I don't like taking the meds,* and he said, *Well you can stop taking them and have an erratic heartbeat, or you can take them and have a normal one.*"

"Tough choice?"

"Tougher than you'd think. I didn't like either choice. He told me it was not necessary to like either one. Only necessary to choose one."

"Ah, these cold-hearted normal people," I said. "Sounds like a Serenity Prayer issue."

"…How did I know you were going to say that?"

"You knew because that's what you say to me all the time—*Find out where it fits in the Serenity Prayer.* Surely you haven't forgotten."

"How could I?" he said dryly. "I have you to remind me."

"*Everything fits somewhere in the Serenity Prayer; your job is to find out where.* And how about…*Acceptance is the answer.* That's another thing you used to quote all the time."

"*Acceptance is the answer to all my problems,*" said Tyler. "*Nothing, absolutely nothing happens in God's world by mistake.* I wonder why I have to be constantly reminded of things that I've known to be true for more than thirty years."

"Alcoholics have overdeveloped forgetters," I said. "You know that. Plus, we suffer from something called Euphoric Recall, also known as Selective Memory. And, Maestro, an enormous capacity for self-deception."

"True," said Tyler. "So pretty soon I'm out there trying to *Be Somebody* because I think it will make me…okay, or at least make me something other than what I am. Less afraid maybe. Whiskey used to do that. A couple of drinks, the fear went away. Vanished…A miracle. Then it was—Let's go get drunk and *be* somebody."

"Meaning somebody different," I said.

"Of course. What's to like about who or what I am? Now I get stuck in self-pity, jealousy, arrogance, the whole gamut of unhealthy emotions. I think that if others only recognized my genius, my wit and wisdom, the applause would be loud enough to drown out my fears. The Nobel Prize would help. I actually think about that sometimes."

"If you had one, you'd probably want two."

"Probably…Ram Dass has a great line—*The problem is that you're too busy holding on to your own unworthiness.*"

"You're standing on Holy Ground, Maestro."

He looked at me for a long moment before he spoke.

"You're right."

"You're a Child of the Universe and, as such, loved."

"…Man…"

If I didn't know better, I'd say he had a little moisture in his eyes.

"Why is it," he said, "…that just talking to another alcoholic can turn a day around in a matter of minutes?"

"I'm guessing the answer is spiritual," I said. "Primary purpose. Magic maybe. Principles before personalities. Carry the message. That's how it all started. You know— Akron, Ohio, two drunks talking to one another. Two guys from Vermont, of all places."

"And now there're more than two million people clean and sober. Maybe lots more."

"A sizeable number. And just because two drunks happened to get together."

"Amazing," he said.

"I think we can call it a miracle and be on safe ground. Nothing in God's world happens by mistake."

He sat back in his chair and took a deep breath.

"You okay on Tradition Twelve and anonymity?"

"I am, Mister Stanley Smith."

That got a chuckle out of him. For awhile, I thought he was going to go serious on me. Tyler doesn't do serious well.

"I think we're done," he said.

"Hurray," I said. "Now we can start on the prison book and become rich and famous. The infamous Stanley Smith will emerge from the murky world of your imagination to take his place among the giant figures in American literature."

"And Edward Bear will become duly honored."

He cleared his throat, usually a harbinger of important information.

"I want to thank you for…listening. For caring enough to ask how I was doing."

"It's a very small thing compared to what I've been given."

Then it was my turn to clear my throat. Guys don't do this…sentimental stuff very well. The best we can usually do is get choked up and embarrassed. Anything's better than crying in public.

"Anyway," he said. "I want you to know that I'm grateful…and I love you."

"The feeling is mutual," was the best I could do. I manufactured a cough. "So we'll get together soon and start the prison book?"

He looked very tired.

"Pretty soon," he said. "A month or two. I need some rest."

"I'll call. See how things are going. You want to talk I'm always available."

"Thanks. I may just take you up on that."

"Maybe you should think about getting another sponsor. Keep the wolves away from the door...The resentments. You know what I mean."

"I'm thinking maybe Tom."

"Tom W, the priest?"

"From St. Stephens."

"...He a good guy?"

"Yeah."

"Tom's been sober a while?"

"Oh, must be thirty-some-odd years."

"But Maestro, a priest?

"It's time I threw in the towel and began to take some direction."

"I'm...surprised, to say the least," I said.

"Time for me to surrender...again. I remember somebody saying: *Life is a series of surrenders.* I never used to believe that."

"You're not going away to hide in some monastery, are you, Boss?"

"Hardly."

"I mean what would Mercedes do? Who would keep her supplied with V8 juice?"

"I'm not going anywhere, Star Pupil. After a suitable rest period, perhaps a journey through the Steps with Tom, I'll be back ready to start on the prison book. At the moment, there's too much of me left in me."

"You know I've got a great quote about that."

"Let's hear it. We'll make it a proper ending to the book."

"This is from Angelus Silesius, one of the early Christian mystics:

God, whose boundless love and joy
Are present everywhere,
Cannot come and visit you
Unless you are not there.

"A perfect ending," said Tyler.

"You think Angelus Silesius was a real name?"

"…Maybe."

"There was a girl in school named Veronica Bunns. Two n's. She had this well-shaped…posterior. We used to call her Magnificent Bunns. Maggie for short."

"Now *that's* a proper ending," said Tyler.

"Can we leave it in the book? This and the stuff about Mercedes?"

"You get to decide."

"I like it, but it's bound to offend some people."

"Perhaps," he said, "some people could use a little offending from time to time. Besides, think of the additional blessings of anonymity."

"Stay in touch, Maestro."

"You do the same. If you need anything, just call."

"I'm going to be calling about that *all our traditions* thing. I'll need a free dinner in the near future. You'll be around?"

"I will. I've decided I need to stay on the earth plane for a while. I have some character defects that need attention."

"Don't forget, we have work to do, books to write. I'm not rich and famous yet."

"Good night, Noble Student. May angels guide your journey."

"And yours, Maestro."

EPILOGUE

So I did some research (read: called Central Office in New York) and found out we were both right. But I was righter. (As you know, I'd rather be right than eat—which is saying something.) Turns out that his edition of the Big Book (which must be a second edition) does leave out the *all* in the Twelfth Tradition. It appears as "*all* our Traditions" in the third and fourth editions. And, since there's only one edition of the Twelve and Twelve, he has an early printing that doesn't include the *all*. New York wasn't positive why it wasn't in there to start with, but in the early seventies it was changed from just *our Traditions* to *all our Traditions*. Which was the way it was originally published in the *Grapevine* in 1949. Go figure. Somebody made a typo and it stayed there for twenty years. Hey, it's not a perfect system. The important thing is that yours truly is the winner.

So now all I have to do is call Tyler and tell him the bad news. He'll try to talk his way out of it I'm sure, but as always, I've got it all on tape. No wiggle room for the Maestro. At least I'll get to meet Mercedes, Tyler's mysterious, bisexual, vampire companion. I'd buy dinner myself just to get to meet her. Maybe I can enlist her aid in getting Tyler started on the prison book. I can hardly wait. Maybe we'll call it Dungeons and Dunces. Fame and Fortune, here I come.

CPSIA information can be obtained at www.ICGtesting.com
Printed in the USA
BVOW11s1559260715

410133BV00001B/45/P

9 781935 052302